The Other End of the Line

WEBSTERLAND
BOOKS

"Well written and sucks you in. Once I started reading I could not stop!! Amazing short story with excitement and surprises in each chapter. Please keep up the writing."
5 Stars, Jamie, Amazon Review

"Such an amazing read. I've read it three times and found myself infatuated with it... I definitely recommend reading this book and grow to love it, just as I have."
5 Stars, Orianna, Amazon Review

The Other End of the Line

"Absolutely loved it!!!! Made me reminisce about "You Got Mail" with Meg Ryan! The story was well told, and the detail exquisite! I connected with Dylan and Bree and truly enjoyed it! It's a must pick up!!!!!! ❤"
5 Stars, Svetlana, Facebook Review

"I was hooked from the minute that I started reading until the very last page. Very enjoyable read that keeps you engaged throughout every page. Great romance novel for all ages. I recommend this book. Can't wait for the next book!"
5 Stars, Yesenia, Facebook Review

The Other End of the Line

W E B S T E R L A N D
B O O K S

The Other End of the Line
Copyright © 2022 by Lyna Lopez
ISBN: 978-1-7343645-4-5
ISBN: 978-1-7343645-5-2
www.lynalopez.com

Library of Congress Control Number: 2022912588

Book Cover Design by CReya-tive
Edited by MK Editing Services LLC

For all of those who fall in love with the acting and are lucky enough to find love with the actor.

Dear Husband

We are here again with new scenes, professional editing, and a brand-spanking new cover! Thank you for
pushing me to accomplish this book and making it better after four years of procrastinating (on my part). I
couldn't have done it without your encouragement—
even though you still haven't read it. (Shh, I won't tell
anyone.)

LYNA LOPEZ

The Other End of the Line

Brina Palace

THERE COULDN'T POSSIBLY be anything worse than watching your undergarments flapping around in the springtime breeze. Waving around in all of its patriotic glory was the school's American flag and my new push-up bra—the one with the extra padding. And as it so happened, a last-minute choice I regretted. Now the entire class would know precisely how flat-chested I truly was as the colors waved around in front of me.

Aesthetically, it was quite a clashing combination to

see the red, white, and blue intermingle with the lavender rose of my intimate apparel. I could feel my face flush bright red in mortification. If the name Brina in permanent marker wasn't enough to point judgmental fingers my direction, the distressed look on my face was enough to tip off the large crowd of students gathering around the faithful flagpole.

I stood amongst the other students of NorthEnd High in abashed discomfort while they gawked at the offending bra I thought was cute at one point—now flew like a vast flapping beacon of dread wrapped in silk. A terrifying heat crept up my chest, only to rush down my spine in a cold sweat. Not to tip anyone off, I brought my head down farther and made my way through the crowded courtyard to the bicycle lot where I had chained my old, burgundy-colored bike beside the rest. The bra was expensive, but I was not willing to claim it at my sanity's expense.

While unlocking the bicycle, I watched my sister Estella speeding around the corner in her cherry red V.W. beetle, with her best friend Ashley riding shotgun. There wasn't a time where I remembered ever riding shotgun in my older sister's car.

We didn't have that type of relationship.

I don't really remember having any kind of relationship whatsoever with my sister other than those random bits where she liked to remind the student body that I *was* her sister when they're caught messing with me. The kids at my school bent over backward not to disappoint her. Such a time popped into my head as I hiked my bag tighter around my shoulders.

In a rare excursion into the popular crowd psyche,

I made an appearance at one of their many post-football-game parties. There, I witnessed the dark side of a teenager, my excellent grades, and varsity cheer squad captain sister included. She stood in the middle of the dance floor, grinding on her quarterback boyfriend in a twistedly sickening display of public affection—and probably where she earned her homecoming-queen crown.

It was the last time I ever stepped foot at an unauthorized school event. Those things weren't for me. For some odd reason, I didn't have the party-mode switched on in my teenage mind like it was for about ninety-percent of the school. I happened to be the average junior who stood in the shadow of her sister's illuminating presence. I considered myself a triple G threat—good grades, gawky, and geeky. I wasn't even good enough for the debate team, an extra-curricular activity I tried to pick up to please my parents. It just so happened that to be on the debate team, one needed to speak up loudly and give rebuttals a lot more passionately, but I couldn't seem to muster up that kind of motivation.

Picking up speed down the hill that took me home, I recalled the embarrassment of seeing my unmentionables hanging on the flagpole as my small, braless boobs caught the wind. This incident wasn't the first time I'd been beyond mortified. Things like that had happened to me before, but this was the first time I felt genuinely bullied by my peers and feeling so bare under my shirt, more ashamed than normal. Shaking the melodrama, I pedaled harder. The faster I went, the better the breeze felt on my overly-warmed cheeks.

The situation should have made me sick to my stomach, but I was undeterred. Girls in my gym class had
played pranks on me before. Nothing new.

I was used to being the classic black sheep in a
modern white flock. My dad was a high-paid attorney
in Back Bay, Boston, where he owned a multi-level
brick townhouse he'd converted into an office for his
multi-million-dollar law firm, while my mother managed a famous magazine as editor-in-chief. Estella was
perfect. Even our dog, Sasha, was as spoiled as they
came. And me, well, I was the runt who always came
up the rear. If I got an A on a math test, Estella got an A
plus. If I earned a second-place ribbon in track, it was
because Estella got first. It always ended up working
out that way.

I took a right at the end of the hill and jumped off
the bike when I made it to our property—the cycle tem-
porarily left discarded in the driveway. While digging
into my bag for the house keys, I saw my book bag had
opened at some point downhill and spilled the contents all over the sidewalk and well-paved street.

"Well, darn."

Papers had scattered all over the manicured lawns
of our neighbors' homes. Running toward the debris,
I picked each item up as fast as I could. Loud music
drew closer, and I knew before I looked that Estella
had made her way downhill in her tiny, red, sporty
car. Quickly picking up a rogue pencil that had landed in a crack in the sidewalk, I ran toward the house
to move the bike out of the way but was too late. The
unmistakable sound of metal on metal, and then the
loud crash of the tipped-over bicycle on concrete rang

in my ears.

"Double, darn!"

Estella got out of the car with an air of dignity, whipping off her Dolce and Gabbana sunglasses. She placed one booted heel in the driveway and then another. She designed the over-the-top move to flaunt her entire wardrobe and flawless look. The deliberate action was like watching a scene in one of Dylan Taylor's movies where the villainess would come out of her vehicle, and all eyes were on her.

I sighed.

Now that was a man worth drooling over. Even though Estella fit the role of heroine or villain in one of his films, the reality was that no woman would ever be Dylan's leading lady over actress Vanessa Dallas. The woman every girl wanted to be, and every man wanted to date. I had never read an article that claimed he had confirmed their relationship, but I was sure there must've been something there at one point or another. The chemistry between both actors was undeniable. They would have made the perfect on-screen and off-screen couple.

"Mom," Estella dragged out in a whiny voice.

My sister's grating voice jarred me from my reverie. It was like nails on a chalkboard that made the dogs howl from the neighbor's backyard. I smiled.

"Bree left her bike in the driveway and let it fall on my car."

My smile dropped. *Yup, always bringing up the rear.*

"Not true," I challenged as I ran behind my sister into the house.

Not that anyone could hear me over Estella's whining and a subsequent door slam. I walked in a few seconds after Estella, immediately pleading my side of the case. Our mother was in the kitchen making an early supper if the smell of oregano and thyme in the air were any indication. Cooking early usually meant she had an important meeting that night and wouldn't be home. Estella argued with Mom, so I searched for Dad, who would most likely err on the side of the evidence.

Dad sat in his study, where he usually hid, talking on his cell phone and typing on the computer simultaneously. My long legs took me to the leather chair in front of his desk, directly across from him. He yammered on at whoever he was speaking with, so in boredom I looked around. His office was a disaster, files scattered everywhere on the floor. The usually neat bookshelves had a few of his law books missing, probably from a case he was working on, and I could tell he'd been a bit scatterbrained. His electronics were even placed randomly around the room in odd locations.

"Brina, baby, are you listening?"

I glanced up at the deep baritone sound of my father's voice. "Hi, Dad."

Dad smiled, lines gathering at the corner of his eyes as he glanced at the door at the sound of women arguing back and forth. I sometimes wondered how our dad felt being the only male in the house. Our mother called out to me. I flinched at the accusatory tone. Instead of jumping over his desk for cover, I stared back at him with piercing green eyes so much like his own. His brow rose in question. The thick eyebrow hid behind a rogue piece of bicolored strands in his usually coiffed hair.

"Do I want to know?"

I sat straighter in the chair while folding my hands in my lap. "Mr. Palace. I present you the case of Palace versus Palace. They are all false accusations, sir. I assure you."

My father sat back in his high-backed leather chair and folded his hands on top of his desk, amused. Seeming to find the black and silver strands annoying, he shoved them back with the rest of the styled group as he replied, "Oh? Please, Miss Palace, present your case to the court."

I did so with gusto. After hearing everything I had to say, Nicholas Palace got up from his seat. His protruding belly rounded the massive oak desk and went out the door of his office. Now safe to move, I followed him past my mom and sister, who were still in a heated debate about responsibility. Emma Palace, super-mom and editor-in-chief extraordinaire, saw her husband walking outside and so she followed. We all went out to see the damage.

Dad took a good look at the bike lying under Estella's car and sighed.

"What in the world is your sister thinking." It wasn't a question, but I shrugged anyway. His boisterous voice rang around the house as he let Estella have it. I could hear the parentals arguing with Estella about responsibility and her carefree attitude. Usually, I'd meddle, and stick up for my sister, but Estella continuously refused to take responsibility for her actions, and I was not about to be blamed for this one.

Not after the day I had.

I took refuge in my bedroom, dropped the heavy book bag on the floor, and grabbed the clicker from my desk. The moment I turned on the television, it lit up to a scene near the end of one of my favorite movies, Celebrity High, starring Dylan Taylor as the sexy male lead. His character in the film was a celebrity who went undercover at a typical high school. Trying to hide his fame from the students, he eventually fell in love with the lead, a regular everyday girl. The female protagonist was a lot like me.

I'd like to think: studious, reserved, and intelligent.

The credits rolled before mom called us to come downstairs to eat. Estella walked out of her room at the same time I did, but with her even longer than mine legs, it took two steps to my four to reach the stairs, and she shoved me to the side with her shoulder.

"Snitch," she practically growled between her straight white teeth.

I bit my bottom lip out of habit but stood my ground as I glared back. Estella was furious at me today, which meant a more significant punishment was yet to come. We made our way to the supper table and sat down. We passed around platters of cheesy mashed pota-toes and roasted chicken around the table. Dad sat at one end, Mom at another, leaving Estella and me to face one another in the contemporary glass-and-metal four-chair bar table that sat in our nook.

We didn't usually sit at the table to eat our food, and when we did, it was generally because Mom or Dad had to work late for the next few nights. They overcompensated for their time away. It didn't both-er me either way what they did. I preferred eating in my room while watching one of my favorite movies or shows, but I was comfortable dining at the table with the parentals too.

I glanced at my parents while stuffing my mouth with one of the delicious buttered rolls. Mom was plenty busy with Estella about an article in one of her magazines as they served themselves similar helpings of vegetables. The two were so eerily similar it made me briefly frown before I covered it up with another forkful of food. Mom's thin, long finger swept back one of the long blonde strands of the chic haircut that framed her face in the front but was cut shorter in the back. Just as my fork came back in for another helping, I watched Estella pull the same move through her equally long blonde hair. Even sitting down, both women were able to make eye contact while I glanced up at their discussion. As I chewed on the creamy mashed *badadoes*, I looked up at my father, whose hair rapidly grew grayer by the day. He sported the salt and pepper look well, which would eventually be me, as we both shared the same dark hair. My eyes made contact with my sisters as I stared around at my family. Her bold stare had me flinching slightly at the accusation still profoundly etched.

"How was school today, girls?" our father asked, apparently oblivious to the tension between his daughters.

I recalled the after-school dilemma and paled. Knowing Estella full well, I snuck a look at my sister, who was practically beaming as she wiped at the non-existent food on her lips. Bi-polar behavior would have to be my diagnosis for Estella's change in attitude.

That, or she did teenage hormonal mood swings well.

"Today went fabulous, Dad. I created a new cheer for the squad, and they simply adored it. I got an A on the math test we had last week, and I helped a new student find his classes today." She grinned when our father patted the top of her head like one would an obedient puppy. "However, my day was dreadfully uneventful compared to Brina's."

And, there it was.

I choked on the piece of chicken I had been chewing quite diligently—my heart pounded wildly beneath my loose shirt. I coughed up a storm, trying to clear my throat as a resolute Estella went into spectacular detail of the flagpole incident to both our parents. Mom was already on the phone with the school PTA, yelling into the receiver about the lack of security in the girl's gym locker rooms, while dad tried to hide the rosy tint that had adorned his cheeks at the mention of my underwear hanging out for the whole school to see.

I could do nothing but relive the tormented afternoon. Estella smirked and batted her fake eyelashes at me the moment Mom and Dad weren't looking. I glared back. Precisely at that moment, Estella's phone went off. She let out a little squeal and excused herself from the table. I sat alone with Dad in uncomfortable silence, watching as Estella left the table with an accomplished smile on her face.

After what seemed like hours, he spoke up. "Brina, baby, are you okay?"

His question caught me off-guard, as simple as it may have sounded. *Was I okay?* I got picked on at school all the time. This incident wasn't the first and most certainly wouldn't be the last. There was a time when I couldn't find my bike. Thinking someone stole it, eventually, the administration found it inside the boy's locker room showers. There was also a time when I went to my locker for some books between classes and opened the door only to have a plethora of enormous hissing cockroaches crawl out of there like, well… cockroaches.

Was I okay then?

I wasn't.

I was hurt then, beaten now, but there was no point in worrying my parents. One more year and school would be over. One more year, and I would be out of that asylum they called an education center.

"I'm fine, Dad." He didn't look like he believed me but agreed to drop the subject. The best part about my parents was that they knew when to leave well enough alone.

A loud squeal echoed throughout the entire house, followed by a more deafening scream of excitement. Ignoring it, I finished the food I had moved around on my plate. I took the plate to the sink, rinsed it off, and placed it in the dishwasher. Mom had finished her phone call, discussing the conversation with dad, when Estella ran into the kitchen on a high.

"Ohmygod, Mom, I just won two tickets to see the premiere of Dylan Taylor's new movie, Breathless."

Dylan Taylor? Excitement bubbled up inside of me.

"Which one's Breathless, Estella?" our mother asked.

I was itching to explain the movie, but Estella beat me to the punch.

"Ohmygod, it's the one where he's this hot, young doctor, and he meets this girl on the subway. They fall head over heels for one another, romance blooms, and then during one of his shifts, his, like, love is brought into the emergency room. She was pronounced dead on the way there, but his love for her brought her back to life. Ohmygod, Mom! He is going to be there for the premiere. I might totally get to meet him!"

He's going to be there also? Oh, wow!

I was even more excited to hear that bit of news. Dylan Taylor wasn't just my favorite actor, but I loved his charitable causes and attitude on life. He never came off as a jerk, or conceited, or even a womanizer. That was hard to say about celebrities nowadays, who spent their money on fifteen cars they would never drive because they had a limousine to take them places. A-list stars usually only held two premieres—one in California and one in Europe. Dylan was from my home state, so he always included us in events that involved him.

"That's good, honey. When is it?"

Estella jumped where she stood, clapping her hands together to emphasize a point. She was cheering even off the field. "Tomorrow night. I'm so calling Ashley. We need to choose the perfect outfits."

That is when my excitement popped and deflated like a balloon that met its end with a sharp object. Meet Bree the balloon and Estella the needle. Of course, she was taking Ashley. I was about to walk out of the kitchen, resigned, when both my parents spoke up at the same time.

"That's not going to happen," they uttered in unison.

Mom took the floor first. "If you want to go, Estella, then you're taking your sister with you."

"What?" both of us called out in an awkward alliance.

"You are still in trouble, young lady. You either take your sister tomorrow night as a form of repayment for ruining her bike, or you don't go. Simple as that," Dad scolded.

Estella paced the kitchen like a caged tiger, ready to pounce. I tried my hardest to keep the excitement off my face but must have failed miserably if my sister's glare was any indication.

"Dad, like, that is so unfair."

"I don't want to hear it, Estella."

"Dad, it's fine if I don't go." Seeing my sister's radical change in temperament, I spoke up. "She won the tickets. She should be able to take her best friend with her."

Mom wasn't having any of the nonsense. "Estella, the choice is yours—"

"You mean I could take, Ashley?"

"—You didn't let me finish, Estella. You either take Brina, or you don't go at all."

"Fine!" She growled and stomped out of the kitchen.

I didn't dare say anything else after that foot-stomping performance. Honestly, I wasn't sure if Estella meant "fine" she wouldn't go or "fine" she'd go with me when she stomped back into the room to make sure she made herself clear the first time.

"I'm not bringing you with me because I want to."

She then stomped right back out of the room.

Message received loud and clear.

I stared at my parents, waved my hand, and walked out of the kitchen, thinking that not only was Estella going to get on my butt about the bicycle incident but about the premiere as well.

Just my freaking luck.

KNOWING I WOULD see my favorite actor, even if it was just a fleeting glance, I woke up on Saturday morning filled with excitement. I quickly tackled all of my chores, got started on some homework, and spent the rest of the morning going through my closet for something to wear. For the first time, I was embarrassed by my wardrobe.

Since I was seven years old, I hadn't worn dresses, and my grandmother had made me wear them for church every Sunday. The majority of my wardrobe consisted of several pairs of jeans. There were tight jeans (because I gained so much weight) in the dresser drawers, ripped jeans (because they still fit, and I

15

couldn't seem to throw them out), and cutoff jeans (because they continued to fit around the waist, but were too short in length).

Because this was an important event, jeans were out of the question.

Going to my dresser again, I pulled out shorts, sweatpants, tights, and a flowery skirt with tiny white ruffles around the edges. I made a face at the worn pattern. Grandma bought me this the last time I went to visit her. I shuddered. The horrid thing was grandma's favorite. The skirt had barely been worn, but I'd washed it more times than I could count as an excuse why I didn't wear it around her. About to give up hope, I opened the last drawer to find some stretch pants—worn pants I used around the house—and a neatly folded black skirt underneath the pile.

Pulling it out of the drawer, I studied the style of the skirt, thinking that the scooter skirt would be perfect if paired with a nice blouse. Estella had bought the skirt during a sale at the department store but had given it to me when she found out it was too big and unflattering.

Moving the shirts around the closet, I paired the skirt with a soft pink t-shirt and reached into the closet for the Mary Jane pumps my mom had bought initially for Estella's college interviews. Estella found the heels "retro." She passed them down to me. I found the heels extremely uncomfortable, so I opted for my pink and black Converse side zips.

Estella would hate my outfit choice for tonight's premiere, but she would have to suck it up because I liked my quirky sense of style. I may not know fashion like Estella and Ashley, but I did know comfort.

Unable to contain my joy, I grabbed one of my Dylan DVDs. This movie was a drama I had bought on sale at the video store. Regretfully, this wasn't a movie Dylan was famous for, but it was my favorite nonetheless. I loved it because it was about a poor farm boy who joined the military to fight during WWII and ended up making a massive difference in the world. The movie was so powerful that I immediately fell in love with the actor. Unfortunately, he was a man I could only love in my dreams, and boy did he star in several of them. The film was one of those roles where he should have gotten an Oscar, but critics and patrons overlooked it because somebody more popular came out with something vulgar.

If he could sign anything, I'd hope it would be this piece of treasure.

Dylan Marcus Taylor

I SMILED WHILE camera after camera zoomed in on me as I reached the old theater. Several people crowded the front with signs with my name "Dylan Taylor" emblazoned on the front in several different colors and embellishments. Cameras from the most expensive to the cheapest camera phones were pointed at my face, blinding me from all their bright flashes. Still, I smiled, self-consciously, hoping I'd brushed my teeth right and didn't have food stuck between them.

That picture would be news. *Hell,* walking to my car made the news. Ever since I became the poster boy for romantic movies, like Fabio was for regency books, the fans and paparazzi were on me twenty-four seven.

Where I ate, what I ate, did I tip the waiter or waitress? What I wore, where did I buy it, who designed it? It seemed that nothing in my life was private anymore. Fans screamed my name while pulling at whatever they got their hands on. The bodyguards did an excellent job keeping the crazed fans off me, but there was still that tiny handful who got through my security.

I walked the red carpet for the premiere of my new movie a few steps behind my costar Vanessa Dallas. I took a second to breathe in her perfume. Vanessa was beautiful, a talented actress, but her conceit leaked from her pores. Women like that drove me nuts. I hated that my fans and the media linked us together whenever they got the opportunity. We may have gone on one date, but once was more than enough.

One supper with her, and I was ready to jump into the soup pot.

These incidences weren't anything new to me, but they still unnerved me. Women would throw their underwear at me as I walked the streets. They'd throw themselves at me, trying to tear at my clothes or cut my hair. I shivered at the thought.

My bodyguard, Brandon, grabbed me by the arm as I teetered precariously after another woman jumped on me—hugging me tightly from the side. Righting myself, I patted her on the back before prying her arms off me and into the guard's strong hands. Still, I made sure to smile as if nothing happened. As if everything was right in my world.

It wasn't.

I had dated several girls. Been connected to several others I'd never met in my life and had arranged secret weddings in Vegas chapels about three different times throughout my career. This world was a fake façade I had to endure because of my celebrity status. My parents were top actors of their time before they died in an accident, leaving the doors wide open for their son, who ended up winning the genetic lottery pool. Inheriting my parents' good looks, money, and acting talent, *Dylan Marcus Taylor* became a household name at sixteen. I started as the lead in a teen series on a family-friendly station, graduated straight to video movies, and became well known for my charming good looks.

Several blockbuster hits followed, billion-dollar franchises. The cinematic world opened to me, but my career had been at a stand-still for quite some time. I didn't hate my roles as the prince, the favorite guy, the handsome young doctor, so on and so forth, but I disliked only being likened to them. If they would let me, I'd go opposite. I'd go for the role of the villain instead of the hero. Or I would choose a movie with substance.

Finally, inside of the theater, with its crumbling walls and the smell of stale popcorn clinging to their dust-layered velvet curtains, I took a long look around at all of the people gathered to see this movie. While my agent Robin talked my ear off about who I should shake hands with and who I should avoid, I smiled and waved at all the adoring fans.

Speaking of those I should avoid, Gabriel Martin

sauntered toward me, followed by his little entourage. Gabriel didn't have as many scenes as I did in the movie, but he played the character's best friend/doctor in Breathless. In many ways, Gabriel was my complete antithesis. The little weasel had slept with various female costars, producers, assistants, and even movie set handlers. The man *literally* worked his way up the ranks, trying to reach the same celebrity status I possessed. The permanently etched grin on his face and those caps he flaunted were going to give me a headache if I had to endure even five minutes in this guy's presence.

"Yo, Dylan. I was surprised when I heard you wrangled the crew to a premiere in your hometown, but I guess when you're Dylan Taylor, you're allowed to do anything." The sarcasm in his words were heard loud and clear.

I turned and shrugged, pasting my fakest smile up for the world to see. "Glad you could make it, Gabe."

There wasn't any way I would allow this weasel to rile me up, especially with all of the cameras pointed in our direction. Gabriel posed beside me for a few more pictures, taking his arrogant ass, along with his entourage, to another side of the theater. My agent talked about business, but I was half-listening.

I could see a lobby and velvet ropes, holding back lucky fans who had purchased or won tickets to the premiere behind. The premiere was usually saved for staff and their families with a few notable people thrown in, except I enjoyed opening it up for a select few fans.

"Go and greet them, Dylan. Some spent a lot of

money to come here tonight."

I put on another fake smile and walked briskly over to the velvet-enclosed lounge. Some of my fans saw me and got up in excited conjunction. It's not that I hated what I did. I loved acting, but some of my supporters weren't excited about my acting skills or what I brought to the art community. They were more interested in whether I wore a shirt in my next movie or who I dated next. They knew everything about me, yet they knew nothing at all.

Some of my films were incredibly cheesy, but they made women happy. Some needed that fantasy man who would cherish them, love them at first sight, miss them even though they were sitting right next to them, and shower them with gifts and candy. I was that fantasy man for women worldwide, even though I wanted a more challenging role I could be proud of.

Finally getting to the ropes, my fans, all lined up in a cluster, pushed one another to shake my hand first or get an autograph and picture. I signed my name repeatedly, then turned and noticed a young woman being jostled around by the others. She lost her balance and fell to the ground. A tall, arrogant blonde beside her stood there and watched, mumbling something I couldn't make out. That had my blood boiling. The blonde smirked as the brunette tried to grasp at what dignity she had left. I ignored the rest of the group in front of me and made my way toward her. She had finally gotten her skirt to cover creamy thighs, but those thick legs couldn't hide underneath the fabric. A genuine grin graced my lips when she glanced up to glare at the blonde.

"Here, let me help." I extended a hand to help her up. All around me, the buzz and whir of the cameras adjusting their lens to capture the moment reached my ears. I ignored them.

She was busy wrapping her skirt underneath her bottom, not bothering to even look up at the person who offered the helping hand. She just took it, and the feel of her slim hand in mine sent a jolt up my arm, spreading all over my body. It was when she stood and swiped at her skirt that she glanced up at my six-foot frame to say something. As was customary where I was involved, she lost her ability to speak.

"Glad you're alright."

The brunette blinked large almond-shaped eyes—mute. Normally, I would be up and out of this particular circle, but the mystery girl's eyes were what got to me, keeping me firmly rooted to this spot. Her eyes were the most vivid green I had ever seen in my life. The girl's cocoa-colored hair fell past her shoulders in wavy layers with highlights that came from the sun, not from a bottle. Her cheeks had slightly reddened, heightening the pink in her shirt. I couldn't help study her as I went from her head to her toes. Instead of finding her in heels like the rest of the women around me, her footwear made me grin even more extensively.

"Nice Chucks."

Those mesmerizing eyes grew wider, glancing slightly at the Converse sneakers she wore. I noticed the innocent expression in those eyes made her even more gorgeous, and it took everything in me to look away. She didn't have to say much to make me want to ask all the questions. If it weren't for the hundreds of people staring dead at me, I'd be doing just that. I didn't realize how lost I was in that gaze when a hand thrust a piece of paper in front of my face. I turned to the blonde who asked for an autograph.

Before taking the paper from the blonde's hand, I noticed the DVD in the green-eyed vixens, and it made my heart stir. It was the first movie I ever starred in that I was incredibly proud of making. Sadly, it didn't create much of a buzz at the time. Ignoring the blonde, I reached for the DVD in her hand, uncapping my black marker. Not even bothering to ask for her name, I wrote:

To my favorite fan, who saw me before anyone else. –Dylan

The delight I felt at the moment would most definitely make the tabloids and magazines all over the world as early as tonight. Cameras flashed from all around me, but I couldn't contain the joy I felt at finally meeting a real fan of my work. Not once had I ever been given that specific DVD from a fan who liked my work. Handing back the cover, I winked at the silent female and moved on.

Still reeling from my encounter with the bright, green-eyed woman, I worked the group. Smiles all around, I signed more autographs, took some more pictures, and made my way toward the large auditorium doors, which opened to let them all inside the semi-lit interior.

I liked filming this movie, but I thought the concept was incredibly naïve and dull. Probably because I wasn't one of the romantics I portrayed on screen. I had never been in love, so I didn't know the power of such a word that got thrown around so sporadically. I loved cats. I loved sushi. I loved. I loved. Everyone loved something. It would be because I meant it if I ever used that word on a woman other than my nana.

My hand shot up to stifle a yawn as I stared at the screen, mimicking the character as he spoke to the staff in the hospital. The actor never really enjoyed the movie like the fans did. After almost an hour and a half into the film, I could hear Vanessa speaking to her entourage behind me. The scene where Vanessa's character falls ill then dies caused murmurs and gasps to come out of the audience below and from the staff behind me. I sat in one of the balcony seats overlooking the bottom crowd, bored out of my mind. One of my phones vibrated from within the pocket of my designer jeans, so I took them out. Placing my work phone on my lap, I took the private line and turned the screen on. It was a message from my cousin Juniel.

I unlocked the phone, clicked on the message, and replied.

A scene on the big screen caught my attention. The moment where my incandescent costar came back to life made me sigh in boredom. The crowd below gasped and cried. My phone vibrated again, prompting me to look at the screen, which again had locked.

I silently laughed as I reread the message I was sure should have meant *Dy*, not an actual signal of murderous intent. Juniel was relentless when it came to autocorrect. My cousin June was pretty much my best friend. I could always count on him, to be honest with me and keep me grounded. Annoyed the phone kept locking on me, I went over to my settings and removed the lock from the messages feature but kept it on everywhere else.

One could never be too careful in my line of business. I went to my phone's journal and typed in my entry for the day. This diary was my reprieve. The only outlet I had for expressing myself and not depressing the rest of the world with my opinions and feelings. I couldn't help but write about my irritation with crazy, obsessed fans, fake people kissing my butt whenever they thought it would get them somewhere, and my distaste for all things phony.

Then those green eyes popped into my mind, so I wrote about the silent female fan with the Chucks. So absorbed at the moment, a hand gripped my thigh, I jumped about a foot up from my seat. The phone slipped from my fingers, bouncing tediously on the rail and then into the crowd below.

Oh, shit!

Rage filled me. I shook off Vanessa's roaming hand and jumped off my seat to look over the rail below. No one stirred or caused a commotion.

Damn! Where the hell is my phone?

If someone got a hold of my phone and read its contents, my career would suffer. I spent my entire life working to create an image for myself that hid my honest thoughts from the public. Not sure what that said about me. I didn't like fake people, yet I had become one myself. I could feel my stomach dip precariously into the danger zone. I suddenly felt nauseous, overwhelmed by the crappy circumstances.

When I focused, the movie credits were on the screen, and everyone moved around me with languid purpose. If I told my agent, I was afraid she'd prematurely go in to do damage control. These phones came equipped with a tracking system. I took a deep breath. All I had to do was find my phone and lock it. Maybe if I sent a message to my phone from the work one, I could get the other person to respond.

Ignoring everyone else around me, I grabbed the business cellphone from the floor where it had fallen.

People milled in and out of the auditorium. I kept the phone gripped tightly in my hand, hoping to receive a reply soon. People congratulated me on another successful film, but my thoughts weren't on the movie. They were on my lost phone, and the havoc someone could play with all my thoughts. Running a shaky hand through my long hair, I stared at the work phone, willing it to ring, but still no response. The delay killed me.

"Dylan, darling, we were fabulous together, weren't we?"

I looked down at Vanessa, who had wrapped her arm around the crook of my elbow, pressing her fake breasts tighter against my arm. She beamed her straight white teeth at me as the cameras pointed at us. I wanted to wipe that smug smile off her face with two quick words: "get off!" Instead, I smiled, momentarily forgetting all about my lost phone, and posed for the cameras with my costar. I leaned over to whisper in her ear.

"You're eating this all up, aren't you?"

She grinned and faked a blush. For the entire world watching, I had told her she was the most beautiful woman in the world.

"Stop being such a sourpuss," she whispered back. People around us would assume we were flirting. They couldn't be further from the truth.

We knew how to fake it.

I was a pro at faking it.

Likely why I hated when others did it too.

ONCE I COULD pull away from the wild pack of hyenas, I made my way to the concierge desk to ask if they had found a phone—careful not to tip-off that it was my phone that had gone missing. No one at the desk had seen anything, nor had anything been dropped off. The missing phone was making me antsy. I made a point to appear at the after-party, but my heart wasn't in it. There I danced with gorgeous models, flirted my way around the groups of the rich and fabulous, but I felt no satisfaction at the end of the night.

People flocked toward me, either intrigued with my fame or money—or both. Some wanted something for nothing. Everyone around me was oblivious to all of the frustrations and anxiety that came with being an actor—all of the times I missed out on a real life because I had an audition to go to or the frustration of re-arranging your entire world to a promised role I eventually didn't get. The entire time, I played phony right along with them. I smiled when I didn't want to and schmoozed when convenient. All for the sake of a career I loved and hated.

I'm a damn hypocrite—the pot calling the kettle black.

The night couldn't help me forget I was still missing my phone. The entire time at the party, I checked my other phone for a response and saw nothing. Each time I went to log into my cloud account, it would lock me out because I kept stupidly entering the wrong passcode. To get access again, I'd have to contact the company that created the phone and get my password reset.

Dread filled me with despair.

I got home to a brownstone I owned in the downtown area. The row house made of brick stood three apartment stories high. Charlie waited for me in the foyer. I petted my dog on the top of his head and walked upstairs to my suite, with Charlie wagging his tail as he followed close behind me. Once inside my room, I immediately sat in the thick-cushioned chair at my desk, running another weary hand through my hair. I was only twenty-fucking-years old. I shouldn't be dealing with all of this stress, and yet, here I am. The person who found my phone would be going nuts by now, getting my private information—my contacts, journal entries, significant events, and meetings.

The things the person would find would be endless.

All of the fake relationships I'd been linked to for the sake of exposure or the secrets shared with me of colleagues in the showbiz industry. In the hands of the paparazzi, I'd be immediately shunned and blacklisted—never to work another acting gig so long as I lived. It gave me a headache thinking about all of the problems a lost phone could cause. Determined to grab the current owner's attention, I sent another text message. Even if I logged into my cloud account to locate my phone, the person would already have had access to every juicy detail of my personal life and probably a few others as well.

I had no one to blame but myself. If I had taken better care, this wouldn't have happened. Lost in my thoughts, I jumped at the rough sound of a knock on the bedroom door.

God, I need to stop jumping at everything.

"Master Taylor, are you well?" I heard from behind the door.

My Nana.

Dorothea Crocker had been my nanny since birth, then my caretaker when my parents passed on. She never left my side and had always cared for me like her own child. If only I could get her to stop calling me "master."

I walked over to the door and opened it wide. "'Sup, Nana."

She frowned at me. "Dylan Marcus Taylor, do not speak to me so informally. Have I not taught you any manners?"

She also reproached me precisely as a mother would, and it brought a smile to my face after the night I'd had. I loved this woman.

"I'm sorry. You did teach me manners. Nana, I am fine. I appreciate your concern. I'm just a little bit tired right now."

Nana briefly lifted the corners of her lips in an attempt at a smile. "Well then, is there anything I could do for you, young master?"

I smiled. "Nah, Nana. I'm fine."

She nodded and walked away. I closed the door. Then left a trail of discarded clothes in my wake as I walked toward my large four-poster king-sized bed. A nice shower would have been kosher right now, but I was way too tired to walk over there. Instead, I placed my business phone on its charger and looked at the empty spot next to it.

Damn, I might as well sleep because come tomorrow, all hell will break loose.

I fell asleep with cell phones and movies on my mind, cursing the invention. It felt as if I had only laid my head down on the pillow when the sound of a loud beep dragged me from my slumber. Eyes still closed, I slammed my hand down on the side table, searching for my alarm clock. I found it. Opening my eyes, I re-alized the room was still dark, and it wasn't my alarm that had gone off.

I sat up abruptly, the sheet falling off my naked chest. I turned to the table and grabbed my phone off of it. Illuminating the screen, I saw I had two unread text messages. My heart beat a million miles a min-ute. Bile rose from the depths of my stomach as fear clenched the muscles in my stomach. I clicked on the first text message.

My relief was instant. The person who had my phone did not get to see anything inside—that's not to say technology hadn't advanced enough to crack my password without breaking a sweat. I tried to think back on the messages I had sent and received and fi-nally decided none of them would tip off my identi-ty nor incriminate me in any way. A function on my phone deleted them often. There wouldn't be many in there.

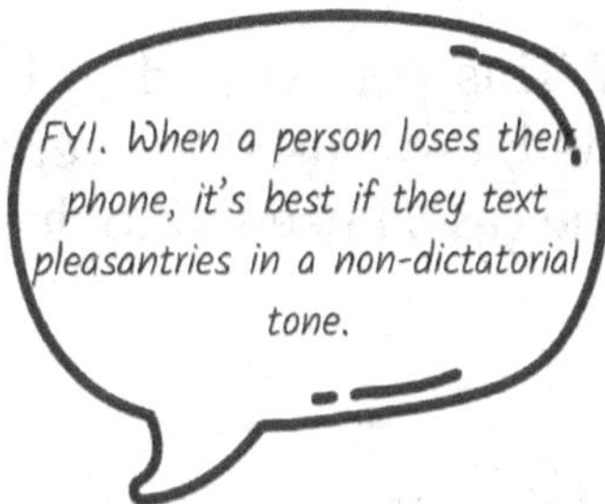

Was this person reprimanding me? When was the last time someone admonished me? *Oh, yeah.* Nana did not count.

Seconds that felt like minutes ticked by before I got a response.

Bully? Now I was a bully? This person had to be female. As arrogant as it sounded, I was used to overly sensitive females. If that was the case, I needed to deal with her carefully.

The phone rang back.

Well, I'll be damned. The female was quick on the up-take.

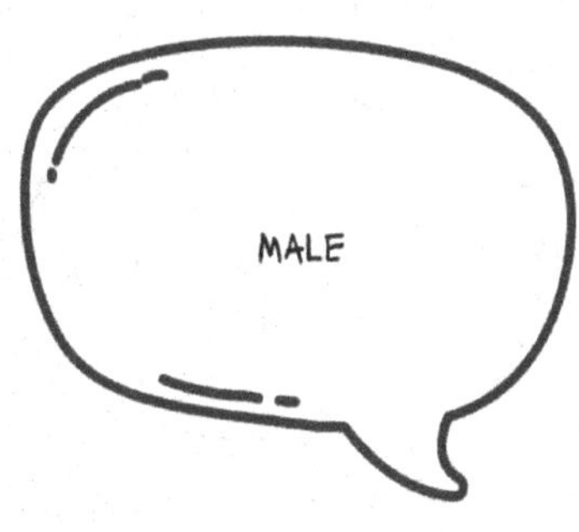

What did my gender have to do with anything? Blowing some strands away from my eyes, I typed.

It took her a while to respond. The anticipation felt like acid burning in my chest.

I dropped the phone on my lap.
Shit!

Brina Palace

I WAS TIRED of being others' metaphorical punching bag. After being jostled by all those fans at the premiere and then laughed at by Estella, I realized enough was enough. If that wasn't sufficient to be utterly mortified, to have my idol come to my rescue was even more embarrassing. Thinking back on his chivalry made me smile, and my heart sigh. Dylan Taylor had helped me off the floor when the rest of the crowd dropped me on my butt. Then he spoke to me. Did I respond? *No.* Did I thank him at all? *Nope.* Like a fool, I had been rendered speechless. If that wasn't enough, he looked at me and gawked.

What if I had something unpleasant on my face? Ugh, too late now to worry about it.

Then he ignored my sister to grab my old DVD instead. Reading what he wrote repeatedly, I wanted to die from the excitement of it.

To my favorite fan, who saw me before anyone else. –Dylan

God, I could die right now, and all would be right in my world. Except, Estella knew how to bring my head back down from the clouds; she sneered and pouted all night. I grinned in the empty room when I remembered the wink before he left.

That wink gave me hope.

Oh, and he complimented my Converse Chucks! A man who knew a good pair of shoes got brownie points in my book. Dylan was even better looking in person than in his movies, which was saying a lot already. Although I had his image to keep me happy, Estella did her best to ruin my night. In the theaters, I tried drying my eyes after a particularly emotional scene, and something hard hit my shoulder and then bounced off the side of my head to make matters worse. I grabbed the object, saw it was a phone, and made a mental note to deal with it after the movie. Unfortunately, I got caught up in the drama that I forgot I had placed the phone in my purse.

After the movie, it got super crazy inside the theater, and I could barely move without getting trampled a second time by people hanging around. Camera flashes blinded me as they took picture after picture of the celebrities hanging around the lobby with their entourage. Estella had left my side several times, getting autographs from Vanessa Dallas and Gabriel Martin. I grimaced.

Estella got a lot more from Gabriel than she planned on when he grazed his lips on her cheek, winking at her suggestively. Of course, Estella got a kick out of being ogled by a star like him. I had to walk away from the horrific scene, leaving my sister to deal with that in her own way. Waiting on the sidelines, Estella finally reached me after what felt like hours, and we both made our way to the car.

I got home, argued with my sister some more, went straight to my room, and slammed the door. Tired of all the drama in my life, I put on my nighty and went straight to bed. After sleeping for a few hours, I jumped out of bed because I remembered the phone was still in my purse. I tried to get in to see if there was information on the owner or the last number I could call, but the phone was locked in every area but the text messages.

What shocked me was that this particular phone model allowed the portion of text messages to be available at the ready right from the home screen. There were messages from five different people, but none gave me a clue about a name or a number I could call.

One note was from a Charlotte, asking the phone owner if they were available a few weeks from now for some work. Another from a Lisa, thanking them for supper. There was an outgoing message from the phone's owner asking a Barron if the car was ready and an incoming from a V.D. asking if they wanted to wear matching outfits tonight. The phone owner responded with a surround "hell no," which I thought was kinda funny.

The latest one was from June, asking if the owner

wanted to party, but the owner was at the premiere then going to an after-party. June had sent back a message claiming the owner sucked and should die, which I thought was rude—to each their circle. I concluded that the owner must have been someone important, but I was unaware of who it could be for the life of me.

I finally responded to what seemed like the phone owner wanting it back, but I was sleep-deprived, annoyed at anything and everything at the moment, and their cheeky attitude just flipped me right on over the edge. The phone belonged to a guy. He could be a part of Vanessa Dallas's entourage or even Dylan Taylor's. The possibilities were endless. The phone vibrated in my hand, lighting up the room in its brilliant glow.

He must genuinely want his phone back.

I could even say he was desperate. Maybe I shouldn't have been so mean, threatening to read his personal information. Something I wouldn't even do if I *could* unlock his phone and go through his stuff. I felt horrible right after sending that long message, but I was sticking to my guns on this one. If I would at least have one person be respectful to me—even if he was a stranger.

I started typing on the screen of the flashy silver phone. A brand new model that hadn't even come out to the general public yet.

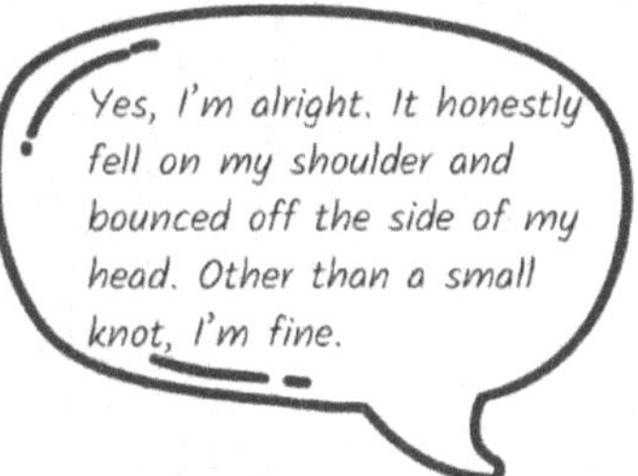

I clicked on send and waited. Luckily, I was not disappointed. The mystery man was quick to respond.

I laughed out loud myself. Looking around my dark room as if it were loud enough that my parents would appear at any minute. It was funny if I thought about it. One minute I was watching Vanessa's character come back to life and kiss her hero—the love of her life—and the next, I'm pelted with a thin sliver of metal. I typed:

The phone vibrated again.

Great. The man was conceited. I lay back on my bed to think of what to do. I wasn't careless and knew I needed to return the phone to its rightful owner as soon as possible. The surprisingly heavy phone vibrated once more in my hand.

I smiled, although no one but the lit screen could see it. The man could play at charming well.

Brina… I backspaced. I didn't want to give him my real name, so I decided on:

Anticipation coursed through my body as I waited for his response. For some reason, I was hoping that he would respond *Dylan*. However, that was way too much to expect for a girl like me. Regular teenage girls like me didn't have that kind of luck. It took a long time to receive a response, and I wondered idly if maybe he had fallen back asleep.

I was right. It wasn't Dylan. But, I did like that Marcus was sweet when he wasn't chewing me out.

Nice to meet you, Marcus.
DITTO, BREE.
COULD I REST ASSURED THAT MY PHONE IS IN SAFE HANDS?
Yes.

A yawn escaped as I rubbed my eyes. I glanced at the clock on my nightstand and saw that it was a little after three in the morning.

I tried waiting up to see if he would respond but fell asleep before I received anything. The following day I awoke to sunshine lighting up my small bedroom. I stretched my arms and legs out from under the covers as I let out a huge yawn. Sunday. I loved Sundays because I didn't have to do anything. My parents took the time to sleep in while my sister left early in the morning to get a manicure and pedicure for her and our dog Sasha. I slammed my hands on the bed, flinching when my pinky knuckle made contact with something hard.

The fan above my head whirred as I wondered what I had hit. Then I remembered the messages I exchanged last night, or relatively early this morning with Marcus, and immediately searched around and under the covers for the missing phone. Finding it, I clicked the side button to awaken the phone and saw two missed messages. Clicking on the first one, it read:

I smiled and clicked on the following message.

The last message arrived about an hour before I got up, which meant Marcus was an early riser. I switched on the phone's keyboard and wrote him back.

I put the phone down and jumped out of bed to get my teeth brushed and some breakfast in my stomach. For the first time in a long while, I ran out of the bedroom feeling giddier than I usually felt. The house was quiet. Running downstairs and past my parents' closed bedroom door, I made it to the front bay windows to see if my sister's car was outside. It wasn't. Today would be a great day indeed.

Whistling, I slid in my socks toward the kitchen and straight for the double-wide refrigerator. Inside, I pulled out the gallon of whole milk and a carton of fresh strawberries. Grabbing a bowl from the cabinet and the cereal from the pantry, I made excellent time fixing myself a bowl of Frosted Flakes with chopped-up strawberries. I made it to the doorway before realizing I had forgotten a spoon and spun around to get it. A little bit of milk spilled over the edge of the bowl and into the runner that flowed from the parlor into the kitchen.

Yikes!

I ran back into the kitchen, got the spoon and a paper towel, swiped the towel on the tiny drops of milk on the rug, and continued to my room. The fan whirred, blowing the white curtains that hung over the dou-ble-paned window. I gingerly placed the bowl of cere-al on my desk and turned on the flat screen. Taking a bite of my cereal, my eyes spotted the load of old text-books the school barely used anymore sitting on top of the desk. I made a mental note to donate them and clean off the rest of the mess of colorful pens spread out on its surface.

When I finished my second spoonful is when I real-ized I had left the phone on the nightstand. I bumped my toe on the bed frame running around the bed. The subsequent pain sent me to the floor in writhing discomfort. Gasping between breaths, I grabbed the throbbing digit. I gritted my teeth as I waited for the pain to fade away. Once it subsided, I let out a deep breath to compose myself as I grabbed the phone and clicked on the unread message.

I smiled again, unaware of how many times I'd smiled receiving a message from this stranger.

The moment I put the phone back on the stand, it vibrated.

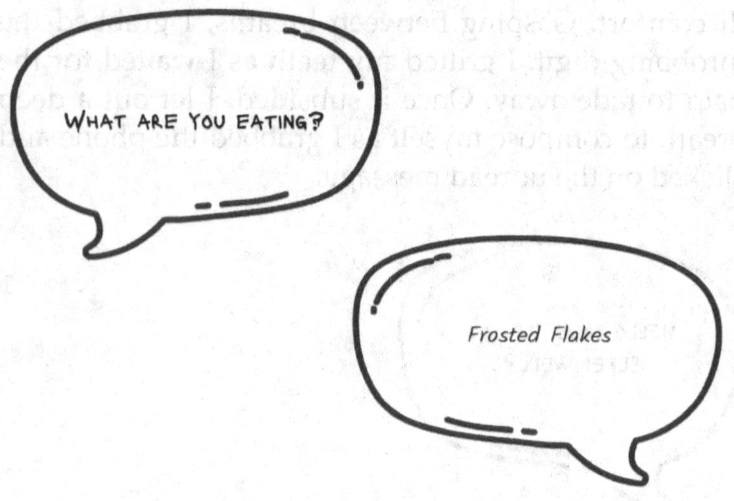

I ran back to my bowl, avoiding the same corner, and sat down to eat. Cartoons played out on the T.V., but all I could think about was Marcus. Was he young like me or an older gentleman? Was he really a guy? What did he look like? I tried to imagine him as a handsome man. Then if he was sexy, skinny, or fat?

For some odd reason, I couldn't help but be curious about the phone's missing owner. I turned around when it vibrated twice. Crawling over my messy bed, I grabbed the phone to see I had a missed message and a prompt showing me that the battery was dying.

I felt sorry for him. He was most likely super busy, and the phone was an essential aspect of his day. The name under his came back as *Work,* so I assumed he at least had his business phone with him, and I carried his personal one. It sucked not to have time for anything and no siblings to terrorize him at the end of a long day. Estella and I hardly ever got along, but I did look forward to the moments when we did. For the first time, I wondered if maybe Marcus was lonely. I wrote him back.

I waited for his response but didn't immediately receive one. Knowing full well the battery would die and then I'd be screwed, I ran out the door of my bedroom, bowl in one hand and phone in another. After making a brief stop in the kitchen to drop my bowl in the sink and pour some water into it, I ran to my father's office. Diving into a cardboard box he kept in a corner with extra chargers, phones, USBs, and other wires and cables he refused to throw out, I searched for something that would fit. Thankful for once my father was a technological hoarder, I grabbed charger after charger and matched them into the phone's charging port. Finally getting one to fit, I ran to the opposite wall and plugged it in. When the screen lit up to charge, I was relieved.

Rushing back to my room, I finished some homework I had left and got started on next week's syllabus.

Mom came up the stairs and into Estella's room for the usual Sunday laundry basket, and a second later, a knock on my door let me know she waited for mine.

"Morning, Mom."

She had pulled her hair back with bobby pins—sans makeup. Even without makeup, her smile made her face radiate. "Morning, baby. Want me to grab your laundry?"

"No, Mom. I did my laundry already."

"Alright, baby girl." She turned to walk down the stairs but caught me before I closed the door of my room completely. "Oh, so how did it go at the premiere?"

I leaned against the door jamb. "It was pretty amazing. He greeted us all and signed my DVD. Definitely the high moment of my night."

Mom laughed. "I'm glad."

She walked away, waving with one hand while the basket of laundry clung to her opposite hip. Nothing else happened the rest of the day. Marcus hadn't responded to the last text that morning, and I refused to bother him. If he wanted to talk to me, he knew where to call. I went to sleep that night thinking about Marcus and dreading Monday morning.

I'D NEVER BEEN more mortified in my life. I walked out of the principal's office with my bra tucked into the bottom of my bookbag. During the day, the principal had decided it was crucial to return the offending bra to its owner. Although beyond mortified, I thought I played it off coolly enough. Now I walked down the hall of NorthEnd High to make it to my next class.

As I turned the corner, I rushed past a group of jocks. One of the jocks threw a football down the corridor to another guy standing right beside me. The ball hit me in the back of the head, sparking a burst of painful illusionary stars. I turned around, rubbing at the sore spot. Estella stood next to her boyfriend,

Stefan, laughing hysterically as her friends pointed— surrounded by a bunch of Stefan's jock buddies and Estella's cheer squad.

Typical that they were picking on me. So cliché to have the cheerleaders and jocks full of misery and mischief. It seemed they had to torment someone during the school year, and this year it just so happened to be me. But what hurt me the most was that my sister would be involved in some of their immature pranks. I had run off in tears before, but remembering the promise to stop getting bullied, I squared my shoulders and blinked rapidly to prevent the tears from falling. My hands clenched. Upset, I grabbed the ball and dumped it into one of the barrels lining the hallway in an unexpected act of rebellion. *Damn, that felt good!*

"What the hell?" I heard one of the jocks call out, but I ignored it, and in self-preservation, briskly walked around the corner and out of sight.

Running into one of the bathrooms, I locked myself in a stall and sat down on the toilet. I rubbed the back of my head, hoping it would take the sting away. This incident was the second time in the past five days that I had gotten hit in the head. I yanked some toilet paper off the roll and swiped at my eyes.

Gah! I hated high school.

That morning I was excited to see that around midnight Marcus had finally responded to my last message. He apologized for writing me back so late, but he got so busy he forgot to check his phone. The mystery man still didn't send me an address, and I wasn't going to push. I told him I found a stand-in charger for the phone, and he was happy about that. For some reason, I liked talking to him. Maybe it was because I had no real friends or because it was an actual guy.

At least, I hope so.

I grabbed the phone, sitting beside mine, from the small zippered pocket of my backpack. Turning it on, I checked to see if Marcus had written me back but only found two messages from Charlotte. One asked if he could get back to her, and the other sent him a number he could reach her at that day. I immediately forwarded that information to Marcus.

Happy to find an excuse to write him, I clicked on the button to compose a new message after sending him Charlotte's messages.

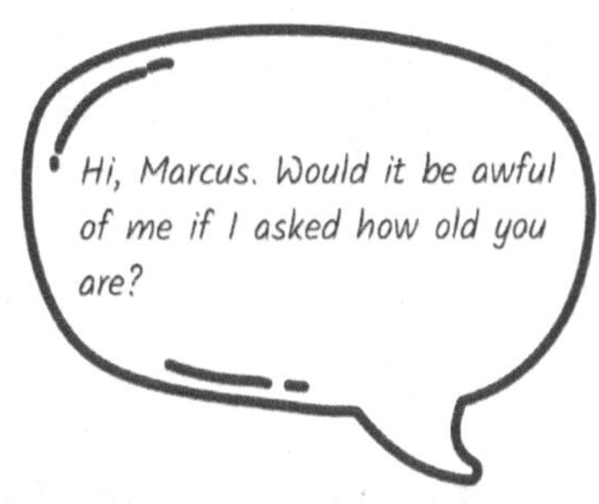

I was about to put the phone back in the pocket of my backpack to head off to my class when it vibrated. Anticipation filled me as I perused the message.

I was immediately ecstatic. My insides flipped around in a frenzy. I bit my lip to keep from squealing out loud.

Not even a full minute later, Marcus responded to my text.

So that meant he was twenty. The sound of twenty was closer to my age than twenty-one. I couldn't believe my luck. That is if he was telling me the truth and he wasn't some pedophile hiding behind the "Marcus" identity. Before I could put the phone back, it vibrated.

Nope, but I do regularly interact with aggravating 18 year olds.
HAHA.
DOES MY AGE SCARE YOU? THAT IS IF U BELIEVE ME.
Definitely not. That is unless you're actually some creepy old guy.
LOL. MY NANA CALLS ME 'YOUNG MASTER'
Hehe. Well, in that case...

I put the phone in my bag and ran out of the bathroom. Marcus didn't know it, but he made me feel better. I thought about all of the things we could talk about, but true to form, right before I made it to class, I slipped on a puddle of soda on the stained floor and landed my butt in a mess.

Darn!

Dylan Marcus Taylor

I PUT MY work phone back down on the desk while I tried to talk sense to my agent on the landline. Bree was a seventeen-year-old girl, which meant that she was either A) one of my fans or B) one of my crazed fans. Either one could get me in trouble if she decided to unlock my phone or realize at some point that I was the famous actor Dylan Taylor. If that happened, then I'd be screwed—no doubt about it. I stared at a photo of Charlie and me playing in the park that sat on my desk in a black four-by-six frame with gold-plated trimmings—a little gift from a director I worked with years back.

Deep down inside, I had to admit I liked this little game I played with Bree. For all I knew, she could be catfishing the hell out of me. But it felt good to talk to someone and not worry if they genuinely did want to talk to me or they were faking it because I was famous. To Bree, I was an ordinary twenty-year-old guy who lost my phone or a weird older man pretending to be a young adult. A smile graced my face, and a throaty laugh escaped. Lately, I'd smiled a lot more naturally than I did before. My smiles didn't feel forced anymore. First with the young female at the Breathless premiere and now with Bree. I was sure she had her questions, but to my luck, she didn't voice them.

I remembered that I was on the phone with my agent. "Yes, I can do that." Robin talked about an underwear contract they wanted me to sign off on. A lot of famous actors did an underwear commercial at one point or another during their careers. I didn't mind.

"That's fine, Robin. I'll see you tomorrow." I hung up the phone just as a knock resounded in my room.

Before I could answer, I watched my crazy cousin June come into the room decked out in designer. The jacket was from Armani, the sunglasses from Gucci, and his loafers from designer Salvatore Ferragamo. June didn't even say a word. He went straight to my laptop and typed in a search.

"Check this out, Dy."

The page he pulled up was a massive rippah in New York for VIPs only. Special guest was supermodel Francesca Petra, who so happened to be June's secret crush. I'd flirted around with Francesca a few times before in specific events we were both invited to but never really hit it off with the Brazilian runway model. Not because I could barely understand anything she said with her thick accent, but because I didn't find her as interesting as everyone else did. I stared at June and laughed.

"June, are you using me to get into this party?"

My cousin may have been a famous perfumer, but he was still no Elizabeth Taylor. He got invited to certain events I made appearances at, but there were many times hosts overlooked him because he wasn't high-society. Because I was an international movie star, doors were open to me worldwide, and my cousin used it to his advantage whenever it suited him.

June gawked back at me and raised an eyebrow clear to his hairline. "Of course! What else are you good for if not to get me into essential parties with vital people?"

I mock-punched my cousin and pushed him off the chair's armrest, where he'd perched his designer-clad butt. The frown on Juniel's face had tears falling from my eyes. "I can get you tickets to the event, but I can't go with you."

June looked put out.

"I have a meeting with a director for another movie that weekend." This movie would be my ticket into a different genre. Instead of the hero, I'd be the villain. "I can't afford to miss it, June."

June let out an audible sigh. "That's cool. So you find your phone yet?"

I couldn't help but smile at my predicament. "Yeah, I know where it's at. Sort of."

Juniel sat down on the edge of my bed. "Cool. So when are you getting it back?"

"I don't know if I want it back right now." I got up from the chair at my desk and walked over to the front of it. I leaned against the wood and crossed my arms over the soft wool material of my shirt.

June snorted. "Right. You call me, freaking out that you lost your phone at the Breathless premiere. Now you know where it's at, and you don't want it back?"

I couldn't help the smirk, picking at a loose thread on the sleeve of my sweater. "Some girl has it. For some reason, I can't find myself sending her the address to mail it back to me."

June jumped up from the bed. "A chick? You got snaps already? Damn boy, you're quick."

I laughed out loud. "No, you idiot. She doesn't know my real identity. She thinks I'm just some guy who lost his phone."

June stared at his reflection in the mirror on my dresser to fix his already perfectly coifed hair. "You catfishing this girl, Dy."

I pushed off of the desk, annoyed. "I'm not catfishing her, you tool. It's not like I told her I was someone else. I told her my name was Marcus. She hasn't asked me any questions I've had to lie about."

My cousin's eyes looked at me from the mirror. He then grinned at what he thought he saw on my face.

"I see what you are doing."

"What am I doing?" I replied.

"She's normal, and you want normal. In fact, you crave it. This is the first time you had an opportunity to be yourself and know that the other person isn't just your friend because of your status. Just..." He shrugged. "Just be careful you don't get hurt, Dy."

My cousin might have been out there in his own world and sometimes a bit reckless, but he always watched out for me. Ever since both our parents died together in an accident, we'd been inseparable. I went on to be a famous actor, and June went into business school. He might not have seemed it, but the man owned a fragrance line, and I was proud to be the headliner in his marketing. It was no problem for me to go around wearing my cousin's cologne to help with advertising. Not because he was my cousin, but because his fragrance line smelled incredible.

"Anyways, I gotta be going. I have an appointment with this scientist about some new ingredients in my new line. Think about what I said, and don't forget to send me those passes." He walked halfway across the room before he stopped. "Call me to go out. I'm free tonight if you're down." June put up the deuces as he walked out of my room.

I grabbed my phone. For some reason, I wanted to hear from Bree again. I searched for her name on my contact list, which I changed recently.

Back in my chair, I rocked back and forth. My fingers drummed on the desk. The phone went off in my hands.

High school. Bree was probably either a junior or a senior in high school. I couldn't recall a time where I was in school. I'd had tutors and in-home schooling for so long I could barely remember a time going to school with other kids. I would have liked to make lasting friendships, mingle with the nerds, date all of the cheerleaders—not that I had a problem doing that now—it would just have felt different being in school with other kids my age. Thinking more about it filled me with nostalgia I didn't know I missed. I decided to take it up a notch with Bree.

I waited for her answer, anticipating her response. She would most likely flirt right back with me. The anticipation made me smile as I waited.

I couldn't help but chuckle. I should've known Bree's response would not be what I expected. My desk phone went off again. After ten minutes of arguing with my gardener about weeds at my California home, I wrote Bree back.

I was about to ask her why when she sent me another message.

What does she mean by that?

My cellphone went off, reminding me of an appointment at the tailor. I grabbed my phone and wallet as I walked out of the room. After rushing down the stairs and almost tripping over Charlie, I snatched the remote starter and ran out the front door with sunglasses firmly fitted on my face. I got into my Audi and off to my appointment, all the while thinking about Bree and what she meant about not being the type of girl a guy would like to take home.

Was she a geek? Or maybe ugly? Did she have some form of disfigurement or disease? The questions pegged me repeatedly, but no matter the curiosity, I enjoyed talking to her. So far, that was good enough for me.

In record time, I made it to the appointment and sat down in a plush leather chair while the designer fretted around with my newly tailored outfits. I took my phone out of its holster while I waited.

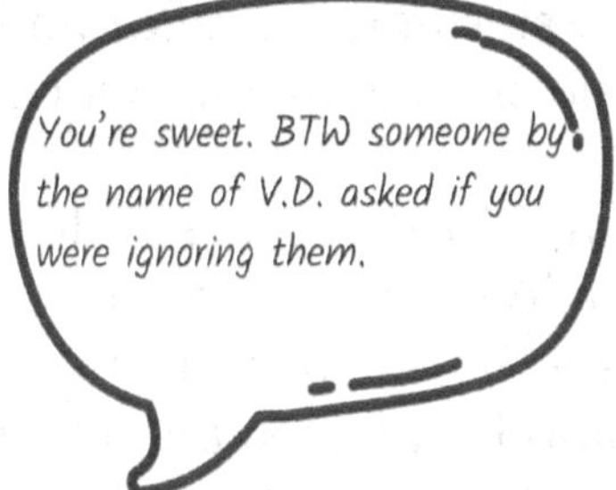

Claude, the designer, walked back into the large dressing room. "Here, monsieur. Try these on," he commanded of me in his heavy French accent.

I grabbed the clothes and put them on one by one, getting the ones that didn't fit fixed and those that did in bags to take home. My phone went off again.

The worst thing I could have done was give Vanessa Dallas my number. Good thing I decided to use the initials V.D. when it came to her. The work phone was used for practically everything under the sun and then some. I only gave my personal number to those who seemed worthy. I hadn't thought Vanessa was as ignorant and childish until it was too late. I wrote Bree the first thing that came to mind.

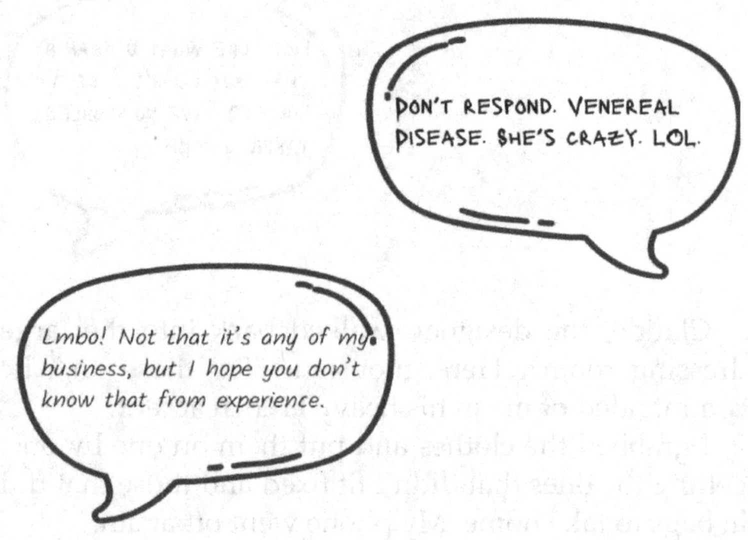

I let out a bark of laughter, startling the tailor and getting a prick from a needle in my thigh. "Ouch, dude."

"If you just sit still, monsieur," the designer scolded.

I grabbed my phone and called Vanessa before she made it obvious who she was to Bree. After a few seconds, she picked up the line, and I explained that I had broken my phone, so if she needed to reach me, do so on this line. Vanessa went into an entire monologue about her fear that I'd ignored her text messages and was relieved that I hadn't. If she only knew. Hanging up with Vanessa and finishing with Claude, I took my purchases and got back into my car.

On my way to my next meeting, I headed toward a small cafe I usually visited for an early supper meeting with a music producer who wanted me in one of his artist's music videos. I got there early, but it wasn't a problem for the staff who sat me in my original spot. While I waited for my guest, I ordered a coffee. In the meantime, I took out my phone.

My phone rang back, but this time it was a text from my agent.

I didn't even bother reading the rest. Robin usually tracked my phone, so she should've known I was waiting for the man to show up. I wrote my agent to ease her anxiety, regardless. The woman was way too high-strung. While sending my agent the message, another one came in.

I got her to flirt. Baby steps.

At that moment, my guest arrived and practically spent the afternoon discussing my role in the video and monetary compensation. I wondered what Bree would say if I told her I was set to star in a famous singer's music video. *Why did I even care?* I'd barely known Bree for two days or so, and other than the fact that I enjoyed talking to her and that she was seventeen with one sibling, there wasn't much I knew about her.

However, maybe I could change that.

Perhaps I could get to know Bree a little better, and then when I was sure she wasn't some crazed fanatic, I'd tell her who I was. Getting the thoughts of phantom Bree out of my head, I got back into the conversation with my guest. With all the plans finalized, I stood up to bid my guest farewell and grabbed my phone to call Robin. Then I checked my missed calls and messages. One from Vanessa, which I ignored. One from Bree saying *okay* to my last text, and one from June making sure I got those tickets for him. I snickered. June was so damn relentless.

I made a few phone calls to a couple of people I knew and got two complimentary tickets to the New York VIP party. I had them courier the tickets to my cousin's house, then called Charlotte about the charity work I was supposed to do next week. That was one part of my life I thoroughly enjoyed. For years I'd helped the foster children of Massachusetts, my home state, and the cancer society for children. I even put up the money for the burn victims wing in the new hospital but made sure to stay a silent donor on that. My fans gave me so much, and it was only suitable to give back.

Wiping the exhaustion from my face, I remembered that Juniel had invited me to go out tonight, which I should have indulged in as tired as I was. A couple of nightclubs in L.A. paid big money to have me show up at their place, so it was better to get it out of the way. There was a major meeting in L.A. I needed to prepare for, so I drove my Audi to the airport to catch a private flight back to my second home away from home. Calling June from the car's Bluetooth, I drove to the exclusive airport uptown.

"Talk to me." June's voice encompassed the interior of my car.

"Sup, June. I'm heading to L.A. Want to party there?" My hand slammed on the horn as a car going too slow in the fast lane decided to cut me off.

June laughed. "Damn, Dy, when you party, you change zip codes."

"You know how I roll."

The phone beeped, indicating another call was coming in. Telling June to hold on, I switched over to answer the call from my agent.

"Hey, Robin. I accepted the offer for the music video. Their office will send you the dates so that you can arrange my schedule."

Her no-nonsense tone came on the line. "Great. Contract's signed by both parties?"

I nodded even though she couldn't see me. "Yeah."

"You heading to L.A. soon? I've got some meetings lined up for you, and I got the call that the plane is prepped and ready to go."

"On my way to the airport now."

She argued with someone before getting back on the line with me. "Great."

Hanging up with Robin, I switched back to June, who was still miraculously on the line talking to someone next to him.

"…head straight there now. Dy?"

"Yeah, I'm here, man."

June said something else; it seemed to his driver. "Alright, I'm down. Heading to the airport now. I'm hitching a ride with you."

I laughed as I hung up the phone.

STROBE LIGHTS OF various colors shone on the dark dance floor, illuminating the people's faces gyrating and dirty dancing in different color palettes. I sipped my third drink, smiling at the beautiful redhead curled into my side. She had her arm tightly looped through mine as if preventing me from floating away from her. June sat in front of me in the VIP lounge, drinking his usual rum and Coke with two blondes on each side of him. The woman next to me leaned toward my ear, suggestively rubbing her body against me. Any other time in my life, I would have gone all for it. It wouldn't have been the first time I'd taken a woman back to a hotel from the nightclub, but I was tired of the same deal with all of them. I was tired of discouraging them from my fame and money, coupled with my looks. I didn't think these women knew how not to be *so* obvious.

"Want to go somewhere more private?"

I could be candid with this girl and tell her she had no chance in hell of making it further than this night. Or I could take her to a hotel and explain as I'm leaving her bed that I wasn't interested in something long-term. Either way, I was still a guy and one with a few drinks in me. Thinking, why the hell not? I was about to respond when my phone went off.

Ignoring the redhead pouting her lips because I hadn't replied, I texted Bree instead.

I wasn't sure why I sent her that last message, but deep down, I must have needed an honest reply from someone not looking to gain anything from me.

As I waited for her to respond, the woman beside me tugged on my arm again. I stared at her and couldn't seem to care anymore. Turning to ignore her again, I waited for Bree to write me back.

Unfortunately, I call it the social hierarchy. You have the losers, including the fat kids and geeks (or what society considers fat). The lame, which consists of the social rejects like kids who get excited about silly things. The 'pretty cool' folk include those with nice enough cars or hot parents, but they still can't be top dogs and the actual cool kids who make up everything the pretty cool, lame, and loser kids want in life.

It seems society has pre-conceived notions about how things should be. That appears to include wanting more than what you have. People go for those with more. If you have it, then it will be sniffed out sooner or later. I prefer the bottom of the hierarchy. We may not be the first pick, but at least we don't harbor illusions about it.

I read the last lines of Bree's text, staring back down at the redhead who was relentless in her pursuit. Bree's words resonated with me. I may be at the top, and others may want to climb that ladder alongside me, but I preferred the bottom with her. There was something about this girl that made me want to do things differently. There was no way I couldn't have any doubts now. Bree was precisely as she made herself out to be.

I never shied away from my gut feelings and wouldn't do so now.

Turning back to the woman sitting beside me, I unlatched her fierce grip from my bicep, excusing myself. Nodding to June that I was leaving, June responded with a slight nod of his head in acknowledgment. For the first time in a long time, I may have been leaving the club empty-handed, but I felt better now than I ever did before.

Finally making it back home after a long day of running all over the place and clubbing with Juniel, I showered, changed, and threw myself on my bed. I turned on the enormous flat-screen TV inside of my L.A. house. My schedule was jam-packed with interviews, meetings, and deadlines. When was the last time I took a vacation? How great would a holiday be?

I did the usual gossip fodder when my agent thought it would be better for my image. I'd held hands with a famous model as I walked a beach shore in Maui, pretending we were on holiday or booked a renowned restaurant in L.A. only to have dinner with the "it" actress of the week. That was a part of my everyday life. I didn't have time to be rational or objective. Unfortunately, *real* wasn't what brought home big fat paychecks—acting did. I fell asleep watching the news and dreaming of cell phones and fans. This time, however, I was grateful for the technology and Bree.

Brina Palace

I STARED AT the graffiti-littered stalls in the girl's

public restroom near the football field, trying hard not to turn around and quit this gig. *Am I supposed to clean this all off by myself?* I decided last year when I started volunteering, that I would help out at my local school. As part of my volunteer work, I had agreed to help clean up the school grounds for the New England Restoration Group I volunteered for every once in a while. A good chunk of the volunteer work hours added up to free credits toward any college of my choice. So, every Tuesday and Friday of the week, and of course for special projects on the weekend, I spent it helping out.

It wasn't like I had a social life that would make my weekends busy or a boyfriend who wanted to spend time with me. Because of my crappy social life, I got to stand in a dirty, disgusting bathroom and give it a complete overhaul. Some new paint, a little floor waxing, new toiletries, and a heck of a lot of disinfectants were what awaited me.

School went fine that morning, except for being cornered by one of the school's most temperamental girls. I walked through the back doors of the school building like I usually did, but the girl stood behind it. I accidentally slammed the door on her. The door hit her on the side of her face and shoulder, and it made her plenty angry. I apologized profusely, but she didn't even hear me. She was seething mad, spewing a few choice cuss words as she pushed me against the wall. I hit my back hard against the brick wall. My heart beat rapidly, afraid of what would come next, but a loud voice echoed down the hall, and the girl looked away from me to my sister.

"Problem?" My sister asked the girl.

Estella smiled at the girl, but there was no merriment, only menace in that smile. My sister rarely jumped in to protect me, but people knew to stay clear when she did.

I couldn't breathe from the fear I experienced, but luckily the girl backed off and walked down the hall—farther and farther away from me. Finally able to exhale, I slid down the wall and sat on the floor to calm down my frazzled nerves. Estella had already turned around to leave. There was no one else in the back hall at that moment, so I thanked the heavens no one got to see me feeling so defeated.

Tears silently ran down my face. At that moment, I honestly hated my life. School sucked. I didn't get along with many people, and most only used me to get to Estella. I couldn't wait to finish school.

I picked myself off the floor, grabbed my bag, and made the trek down the hall toward my first class. I had to help the teacher pass out students' old worksheets in class, and while walking down one of the rows, one of the boys stuck his foot out and tripped me. Whether it was intentional or not, I was a magnet for disaster. The action sent me flying down the row into one of the desks, which happened to belong to one of the most incredible guys in my junior class. Students laughed loudly, especially when the guy whose desk I ran into jumped back, alarmed as if I had a rare flesh-eating disease. The teacher came around to help, shushing students along her way. I wanted to hide under a rock. The blood in my face exploded because all I could feel was heat coursing through me.

"Who tripped her? Mr. Alexander, was it you?" the

teacher yelled.

"Mrs. Carlson." I was not about to get harassed by the students if Jake Alexander got in trouble for tripping me. "It was my fault. No one else's. I wasn't looking where I was going." I could see Jake take a visible sigh of relief while the rest of the students looked at the teacher to gauge her reaction.

She didn't seem to buy my excuse but decided to drop the subject. "Fine. If you insist, Miss Palace."

I only nodded.

After that incident, the day went relatively well. Lunch had come and gone with no problems at all. Then as I was about to pack up the rest of my lunch, the cell phone in my back pocket went off. I pulled it out and read the message Marcus had sent me.

I giggled. I enjoyed my talks with Marcus because he made these dreadful days fun.

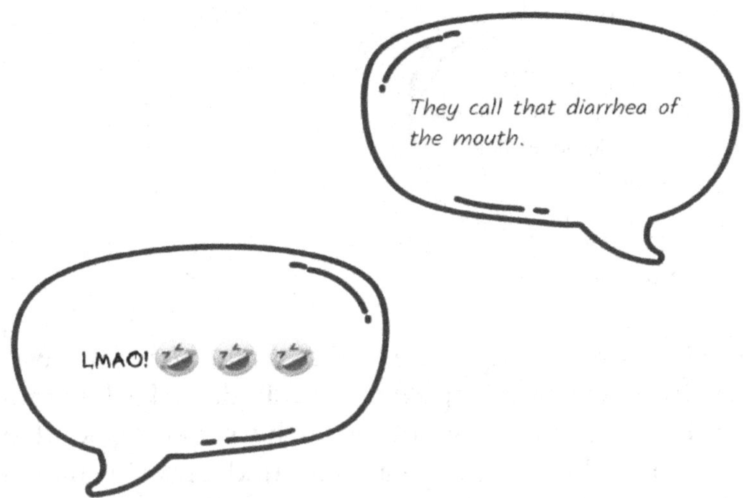

I would have loved to see his smile or hear his laugh. It made me imagine what it would look or sound like.

I anxiously awaited his response.

His words brought me to fits of laughter. That was one thing we hadn't spoken about in days. I asked him for his address on Sunday, but he never responded with one. Then Monday came around, and we chatted like old buds. Not that I complained. Talking to Marcus had been enjoyable and a great distraction from my mundane existence.

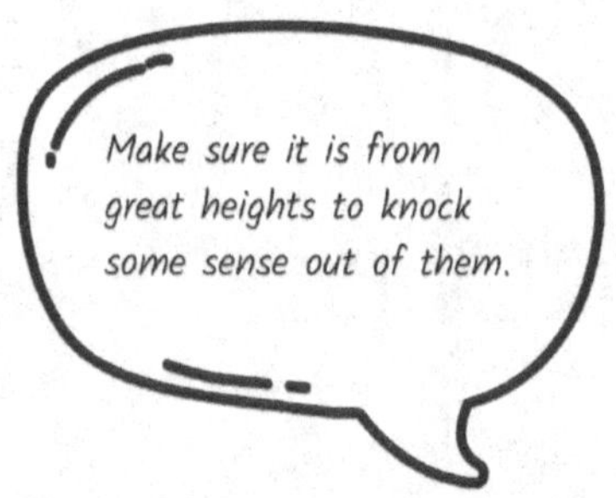

I got up and threw away the rest of my lunch while I waited for him to respond. It took him longer than he usually did, so I walked to class instead. Before getting there, the phone vibrated in my back pocket. I gladly pushed my bag higher up my shoulder to fish out the phone.

It made me so happy that I almost missed that first step inside the building.

Placing the phone back into my pocket, I ran inside in time for the first bell. The rest of the day went by quickly after that. Now I stood inside of the field bathrooms contemplating my next step, secretly hoping Marcus would come to my rescue. I grabbed a sponge and bleach and went hard against the walls and stall doors. The bathrooms weren't huge, but they still got dirty very quickly. As I scrubbed the walls, I watched the graffiti melt together in a puddle of garbled words.

After I washed all the walls, I picked up the paint and got to work on the stalls—turning them from a washed-out yellow into a dull rose. I polished the faucets and used cleaners in the sink and counters.

I walked back out into the warm, breezy night toward the supply shed held on the school grounds. Once inside, I placed the rest of the paint and washed brushes in their respective spots, moved the floor buffing machine and some specific chemicals, and made my way back out to the bathroom. There I bumped into Cassidy, one of the other volunteers for the New England Restoration projects who was finishing up with the boy's bathroom.

"Hey, Bree. You get the girl's room done?"

I stopped walking to face Cassidy. "Yeah, I'm just going to get the floors waxed, and then I'm heading home."

Cassidy grinned a mouth full of braces. She was a freshman in college. Sweet girl, but like me, she mostly kept to herself.

"Cool, you mind bringing that bad boy to my end after you're done using it?"

I started walking again. "No, problem. Will do."

I barely heard Cassidy's thank you as I walked into the bathroom, which now smelled of fresh paint and bleach. As soon as I finished with the floors, I happily brought the machine to Cassidy. Knowing there wasn't much more I could do for the bathroom, I posted a sign keeping people away from it and locked the door.

I then made the long walk back home with thoughts of Marcus dancing around in my head.

Dylan Marcus Taylor

MY EYES GLAZED over as I finished meeting after meeting in a constant non-stop loop with no end in
sight. I thought my Tuesday was busy, but Wednesday
took the cake. My team ushered me from one spot to
another to meet and greet fans, speak with new clients,
sign contracts, meet with my lawyers and accountants,
and now I had to do my first commercial for Indigo underwear. That wasn't all. The ridiculousness of underwear modeling made the men look naturally pumped
and proportionate while wearing their underwear.
Instead of taking a shower to get ready, the assistant

director pushed me into a small gym and told me to work out hard for the next forty minutes.

That was what I did before I walked out on set, out of my sweaty gym clothes, and into some freshly pressed Indigo boxer briefs. The muscles in my arms throbbed unmercifully, and my abs formed symmetrical rips. Every time I took a breath, each muscle in my body stood out. A tiny Asian girl came up to me with a spray bottle of water and baby oil. She spritzed the mixture all over my body. Some went in my hair to give it that shiny wet look. She ran her fingers through the thick mass of hair.

The woman practically purred as she said, "I'm a big fan, Mr. Taylor."

I smiled for her and thanked her for her support, then walked toward the set and female model they had waiting for me. After two hours of tedious posing and re-posing, I finished for the day. With no showers handy to clean the mixture off, I put my clothes on over the sweat-mixed oil and drove home in the Maserati I owned while in L.A. It was about six-thirty at night before I got in. I walked into my lit bedroom to see two pieces of luggage sitting half-empty on top of the bed. With the sound of humming coming from the closet, I turned in that direction.

I found my Nana had flown in from Boston and was rummaging through my wardrobe. She had a crisp multi-lined button-down in one hand and was looking at one of my Fedoras in the other. Assuming she didn't find it proper for the shirt, she put it back on the rack dedicated to all my hats. I had a stand, shelf, or island exclusive to every single piece of my wardrobe. The walls in my closet were lined with clothes, all in order by style and color combination. The back wall was full of row after row of shoes and several islands throughout the closet's interior that held all of my accessories from jewelry, to cuff-links, to scarves. The New England bedroom closet was extravagant, but the one in my L.A. home was beyond impressive.

"Oh, you scared me, young master," Nana exclaimed in a breathy voice.

I took a good look at my Nana with her bi-colored bun and smiled. She seemed so fragile with her tiny hand clutching at her chest as if to keep her fast-beating heart from jumping out. Nana stood in front of me in her long black skirt and white button-down shirt with spectacles that sat at the tip of her nose. All I could see at that moment was how much I truly loved this woman. From the moment I became a star, she protected me from the riffraff (she referred to my so-called friends) and the hussies (a term she used for the women who clung to me like glue) who tried to achieve something for nothing, especially from me.

I walked over to her and wrapped my arms around her tiny frame, holding her tightly to me. The entire world around me could come crashing down, but within the fold of her arms, it felt like nothing could touch me.

"I'm sorry, Nana."

She hugged me back for a moment then pulled me away from her while running her nimble fingers down my shirt to loosen the wrinkles like she always did.

"You should be, young man. Now go on and take a shower because you smell like sweat, and..." She took a deep whiff. "Is that baby oil? Why do you smell like a baby's butt?"

I grinned.

"Nevermind, I do not think I want to know," she exclaimed while shaking her head.

I laughed as she hurried out of the closet to put the clothes in my suitcase. My phone went off as I walked out of the closet. The melody bounced off the doors of the cabinets. I placed a dedicated tone for all messages that came from the phone Bree had.

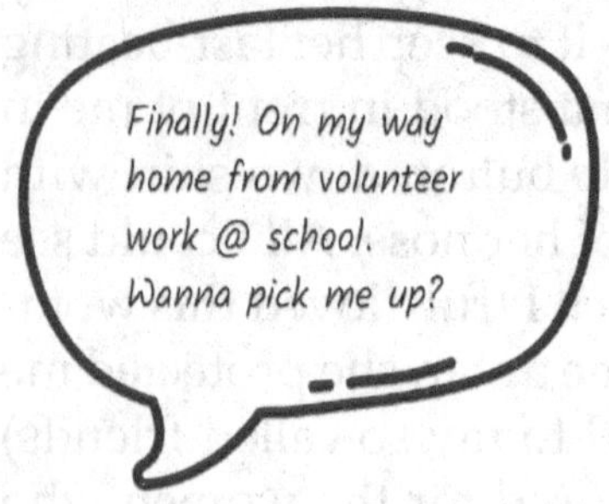

I laughed silently to myself, knowing full well I had the cheesiest grin on my face. From Bree's message, I was able to find out at least that she was a volunteer like me. This bit of news was a positive in the sea of all the negative crap in my life. I enjoyed my talks with Bree. They helped me pass the time and think outside of the usual box I found myself stuck in. I didn't have to worry about her being a gold-digger because she didn't know my real identity, and I genuinely enjoyed her jokes and teasing personality. Taking a chance on her, I hoped to God that she was who she said she was. Like the internet, people can be incredibly deceiving when they aren't facing the truth. For some reason, call it wishful thinking, Bree seemed genuine to me.

I turned to walk out the door when I stopped in front of Nana, who curiously watched me from her spot by the bed. There was a moment of complete silence before I could no longer take it.

"What?"

She clucked her tongue. "Either Mister June put that blush on your cheeks, or a young lady did—" she shrugged "—or old. Whatever tickles your pickle," said the saucy old coot.

All I could manage was to shake my head and wiggle my finger in her direction. She could always see right through me and still manage to crack jokes. I didn't know what was going on with Bree and me. All I knew was that I didn't want it to end yet. The moment I sent her the address to mail the phone, it would. I walked across the room to a chair that sat by the far end of the wall. There I pulled off my shoes and stood up to take off my shirt, which I threw at Dorothea. She managed to catch it one-handed. Nana clucked at me again, and just as I was about to take off my belt, the phone went off.

Movie night?

This moment right now might be the perfect opportunity for me to steer the conversation more toward who I was to see if she was a fan of my work or a crazed fan in general. Unless she indeed was one of the rare teenage girls who had never seen my movies—the premiere being her first. I sincerely hoped it was the former and not the latter choice. Being judged for just Breathless would be horrible for me as an artist.

I got my belt off but didn't even get to unbutton my jeans before the phone went off again.

I didn't know if I wanted to kiss Bree at that moment or smack her across the head. How could she say she loved my acting and still managed to ruin the mood by saying that I had great chemistry with Vanessa in the exact text? I took off my pants, leaving them in a pile in front of the chair, and made my way into the bathroom in the Indigo brief shorts from the photoshoot while Nana packed my clothes for the upcoming trip overseas in the background. I walked inside and closed the door. Turning on the shower, I could hear Nana yell at me from behind the door.

"Don't forget to wash behind the ears, Dylan."

I smiled. This woman was like a mother to me. I made sure to do just that as my muscles quivered under the hot water spraying my body from different angles.

Sigh. Another day over.

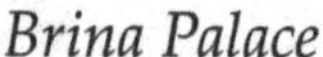

FINALLY FINISHED WITH the last editing marks I needed to accomplish for my English essay on Shakespeare's *Macbeth*, I grabbed the control from the top of my desk to turn on the TV. I always watched Gossip weekly—a show on AFN that aired every Friday at eight. This program recapped all the new movies coming out, new actors and the like, who left who, and every other gossip in the entertainment business you could think of to hear. The host, Penelope, was very good at her job. She had people on her program all the time and got them to divulge in one form or another information they weren't ready to share. I put my papers away and the pencil back in the cupholder when the familiar sounds of the show's intro music came on.

Penelope looked fabulous on-screen in a red two-piece suit as she greeted her fans in the audience and those sitting at home. She said something I didn't quite catch because I had my head in the closet to put my bookbag inside. When I turned around, I saw a picture of Dylan Taylor on the show's primary monitor. It was a photo taken on the Breathless premiere red carpet in Italy.

His gorgeous dark locks complemented the long tweed overcoat by Dolce and a Paul Smith wrap scarf. My sister had recently looked at the same scarf to buy for her boyfriend for his birthday, but it was too expensive. Dylan's hair was long and slicked behind the ears. His dark eyes hid behind thick black eyelashes and dark eyebrows. He was simply beautiful. I quickly ran over to the control and put the volume up on the TV.

Host Penelope Samson addressed the audience. "Today, we have a huge treat for you guys. Who here can tell me who that handsome devil on the screen behind me is?" The show's audience went nuts as they screamed Dylan Taylor's name.

"That's right! Everyone give a warm welcome to Dylan Taylor."

The audience screamed. I sat eagerly on the edge of the bed. Over the show's loudspeakers, Dylan's voice could barely be heard over the roar of the crowd. "Thank you for having me on your show."

His voice thrummed the blood in my veins like the strings of a guitar.

"Dylan couldn't be here with us today because he is overseas meeting with some significant people," Penelope added.

"That's right," he responded.

"Now, Dylan, is it true that you have just signed off on a new movie deal with director Steven Berg and new French producer Jacque Dion?"

Dylan laughed. "That's true, Penelope. I have just signed on to make a new action film with them. I'm so excited to be filming with such talented personalities like Steven and Jacque."

Penelope crossed and re-crossed her legs. "Dylan, girls are obsessed with your romantic movies. How do you think they'd feel about you appearing in an action flick?"

"Haha. I hope that my fans will enjoy this movie as much as they enjoyed the others. I'm working with extremely talented actors and remarkably professional staff. I could only promise my fans that I will try my hardest not to let them down."

He would not let me down. To be in an action movie with Berg, who had done several inspiring and incredibly excellent films, and Jacque, who had produced only two films but both were smashing successes.

"I have a question for you, Dylan. If you don't mind." Penelope flirted with the camera as if flirting with Dylan himself.

"Shoot."

She smirked coquettishly. "So, are you dating anyone right now? Someone by the name of Vanessa Dallas, maybe?"

He laughed out loud, which sent my heart thumping a Texas two-step. "No. I'm sorry to disappoint, but I'm not currently dating anyone. I care about Vanessa as a dear friend, but we are not together."

Relieved, I sighed. Not that it would matter either way because Dylan Taylor didn't even know I existed. I also felt guilty, because in a way, I had a "thing" with Marcus. *Ugh. Why am I making things so confusing?* Marcus is just another person on the other end of the line who had never met me in person and could even be a creepy eighty-year-old guy passing himself off as a young twenty-year-old for all I knew. Then, on the other hand, I had Dylan, who didn't know I existed, and if he did, he would probably pick me off like gum off his hundreds of dollar shoes.

"So, when are you coming back to the states?"

I focused on the television screen, attentively trying to hear what Dylan would say next.

I could see the smile Dylan had as he spoke. "I'll be back home in the states in a couple more days. Just have to wrap a few things up, but I will be back in time for my cousin Juniel Taylor-Lemore's unveiling of Sheik in New England."

The host animatedly clapped her hands together. "That's right! Folks, we have a great surprise for those of you at home and our audience members today. Juniel Taylor-Lemore has personally sent goody bags to every one of you in the audience today, as well as a free sample of his new perfume, Sheik."

Everyone feverishly clapped and hollered their glee. "You are getting Juniel's perfume before it even comes out!" she yelled. "For those of you watching tonight, you have a chance of winning two free tickets to be there at the unveiling." Another round of applause erupted throughout the audience.

"Dylan, would you like to explain the winnings to whoever our lucky caller is?"

Dylan Taylor snickered. "I'd love to, Penelope. The lucky winner will get two free tickets to join Juniel Taylor-Lemore at the unveiling of Sheik, taking place at the New Seasons Boston Resort. You will have all accommodations paid in full."

"Juniel Taylor-Lemore is the hottest new fragrance guru right now. He came out with his first men's cologne Zeus just a couple of years ago, followed by D'artanian—Dylan's personal favorite, which he launched here in California."

Dylan laughed in the background.

"Then he switched things up and came out with his first line in women's perfume, Lush, and is now introducing Sheik as part of his East Coast brand."

"You're correct. Juniel's cologne is one I do not mind wearing at all. The chemicals are non-irritant, and it smells fantastic."

Penelope giggled, sending a wink at the camera. "Dylan Taylor, thank you so much for spending some time with us today. We know you are a very busy man."

"It was a pleasure. Thank you for having me," Dylan replied.

"Stay tuned because when we come back after these brief commercials, we will be telling you at home how to win."

Excitement bubbled through me like a geyser. I ran over to my desk to finish stacking up my books and study guides. In the background, I could hear commercials with talking dogs and geckos explaining the benefits of certain foods and the importance of insurance. I took a sip of water when the show's theme song came back on. I immediately rushed over to the TV but tripped on one of my discarded sneakers, causing me to faceplant on the bed. I heard the host welcoming everybody back to the show.

"I know you are all dying to know how to win, so listen close. When you hear this sound—" a buzzing siren went off in the studio "—call the number located at the bottom of the screen. Be our fourth caller in appreciation of Juniel Taylor-Lemore's fourth fragrance. Don't change that channel because the next winner could be you!"

I could almost feel the host pointing her finger as if pointing it directly at me. I knew it was ridiculous because there were probably thousands of people watching her show right now. A girl could dream. Penelope Samson continued with the show, explaining important entertainment events that were coming up and new must-see movies. More minutes and commercials went by as she explained who all the latest hot actors and actresses were, who was dating who, and who had recently broken up. Penelope then explained the argument between two superstars who couldn't watch what they said on Flippant, a social media outlet, and another one who couldn't stay out of everyone's business. She was about to say something about the hottest bodies on the beach when a siren went off in the studio.

I immediately jumped into action. I pulled out my own cell phone and dialed the number on the screen. The first time I phoned, it gave off a busy signal, but I redialed faster than my fingers knew how to process. I got a ring, then another, before someone picked up and placed me on hold. On the television, I could see the excitement in the audience.

"Thank you for calling. What's your name, caller?" Penelope asked.

A young female voice came out of the loudspeakers. "Brenda. Did I win?"

Penelope pouted. "No, Brenda. You were our first caller. Thanks for trying." Another caller went on air, and she, too, lost being the second caller of the night. The third person on air was a guy who was thanked for trying and was close but did not win.

I held my breath in anticipation when someone

picked up the other end of the line. I could hear the open air and movement on the line. Then I heard Penelope's voice on the other end asking me for my name."

"Bri…Brina Palace," I stuttered.

Sounds of applause went up in the audience. "Congratulations, Brina Palace! You have won two tickets to the unveiling of Sheik. Please stay on the line, don't hang up!" She smiled while pointing her finger at the television screen, and this time I knew that it was for me.

Now, all I had to do was wait on the phone and not pass out.

AFTER WHAT SEEMED like hours waiting, but were only minutes, a voice came on the line that sounded like Dylan Taylor. My teenage heart descended into the pits of my stomach at the thought that he was on the line only a mere breath and a whole lot of miles away from me.

"Congratulations, Brina Palace. My name is Juniel Taylor-Lemore."

I could die. Juniel Taylor-Lemore, the fragrance phenomenon of the twenty-first century, was talking to me. He was also Dylan Taylor's closest living relative. "Oh, sweet Lord Jesus, is this a recording?" This moment could not be happening to me. My idol crush's cousin was talking to me on the phone—a famous perfumer was about to invite me to a party. I giggled at the surrealism of it all.

I heard a laugh, so similar yet so different, respond to my amusement. "No, it's not a recording. I really wanted to speak to the winner personally and congratulate you myself."

I squealed, jumping on my bed. "Mister Taylor-Lemore, I love your perfume, Lush. I bought a bottle a couple of months ago and have already used it up. I'm a big fan."

Juniel laughed again, pleased with my outburst. "I'm so glad. This bit of news makes the wins that much better, Brina, but please call me June."

My heart froze. *Now, why did that name sound so familiar to me?* Ignoring the weird sensation, I said, "So long as you call me Bree, Mr. June."

We spoke about my win a little longer and then went into specific details about the rest of the winning package. Because Juniel was a native of New England, he and Dylan always made sure to make movie premieres and events in their home state and Los Angeles. Luckily, we were from the same place and grew up around the same things, so we had a lot to talk about. For the first time, I wasn't afraid to speak to someone. June had a warmness about him that made it impossible to be scared. I gave him my address when he asked.

I opted out of the hotel accommodations because I was a New England native and underage, which meant I could not stay in a hotel without an adult over eighteen. Hence, June and I settled on a limo coming to pick my guest and me at my home. We laughed about the silliest things as we spoke, making me feel that our light banter was closer to a flirtatious friendship. Finally hanging up, I ran out of the room, tripping over my dog Sasha, who growled at me in response, and down the stairs to my parents' bedroom.

Mom had recently returned home from work, but dad was still missing in action. I told her all about my win. Mom was equally excited for me because it meant exposure for her magazine agreeing to let me go. Getting her permission, I ran back upstairs to tell Estella.

Estella and I fought all the time, but I still unconditionally loved my sister, and I knew in her weird way she loved me too. Plus, it was only fair that I took Estella, seeing as she took me to the premiere of Breathless. I knocked on the door and pushed it open, instantly greeted by the strong scent of nail polish.

"What?" I heard Estella call out as I took in her feminine room.

Estella had pink and baby blue colors all over her room, rivaling my more comfortable white walls and floral bedding. She didn't even look at me as she concentrated on her toenails. I wasn't sure why Estella painted her nails when she would get them done on Sunday anyway. It was the little quirks like that that made us so different from one another.

I snapped back into the present. "I wanted to let you know that I won some tickets to the unveiling of Juniel Taylor-Lemore's perfume Sheik and I wanted you to be my plus one."

At that, Estella's head snapped up. Her long blonde locks flipped back behind her shoulders from the sheer force. "Are you kidding?"

I smiled. "Nope."

Estella had a calculated look on her face as she asked, "Why are you asking me? Is this some twisted trick or something?"

I could see where she'd probably think that, seeing as most of the time, we barely managed to get along. But, fair was fair. Estella had to give up her ticket; it was only fair I did too. "You had to give me your extra ticket to Breathless; it is only right that I do the same," I whispered honestly.

Estella was quiet for a second before an excited "yay" ripped through the air. "Oh my god, I have got to call Ashley!"

I didn't even wait to get ushered out of the room. The moment Estella grabbed her cellphone to call Ashley was the right opportunity to step out. As I closed the door to my sister's bedroom, I could hear her animatedly talking to Ashley about what I had told her and where she was going. Feeling like I had done my good deed of the day, I ran to my room and straight for Marcus' cell phone. A grin adorned my face when I saw I had one missed text from him.

I glanced over at the clock on my nightstand. It was

only a little after nine at night. Why would I be asleep? Not that I could sleep now with all the excitement bubbling up inside of me.

Three in the morning? That's right! Marcus mentioned before that he was going overseas for a meeting. It was sweet of him to think of me at that time or foolish that he was awake instead of taking the opportunity to sleep.

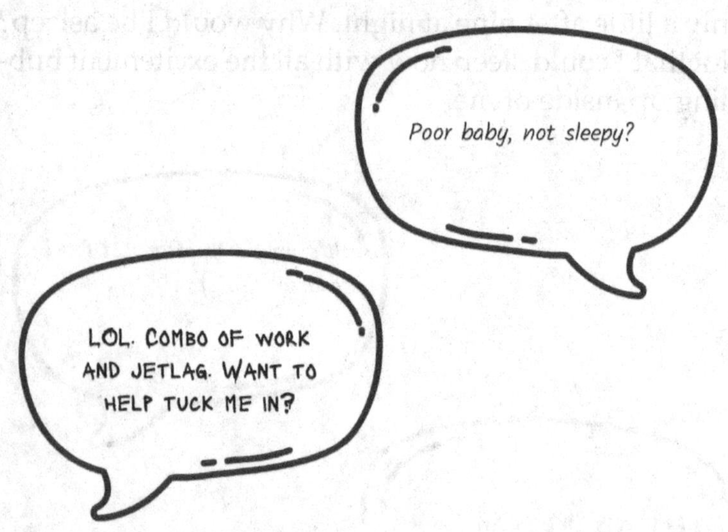

I instantly blushed. Marcus always made me feel in some indescribable way. I remembered a lullaby my mother used to sing Estella and me to sleep at night and started typing it.

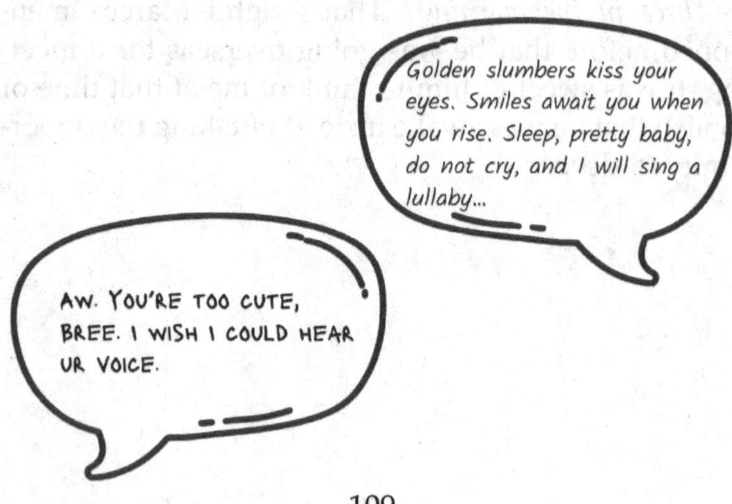

My cheeks burned as blood pooled there again. I fanned myself with my hand. My cellphone dinged with an email from June's press group with all the information. I bit my lip. This moment didn't feel like it belonged to me. Good thing Marcus couldn't see me because I blushed more with him than I had with anyone else. Ever. Marcus made me feel special even though our conversations were brief and our time together short. I didn't know what to say, so I debated between humor and honesty.

I didn't sound like Jay Leno and Fran Drescher's baby, but my voice was different than other girls. Some were overly feminine. I had a huskier tone. More like I was about to lose my voice. Marcus' phone went off again.

His words reminded me of the times I had sung it with my mother, sitting on her lap, comforted within the folds of her arms. There were many nights she'd lie awake with us as she sang us the lullaby to ease our worries when we felt ill. Being wrapped in our mother's arms as she rocked us back and forth was a memory I'd carry with me always. Estella and I were older. We spent sick nights in bed alone.

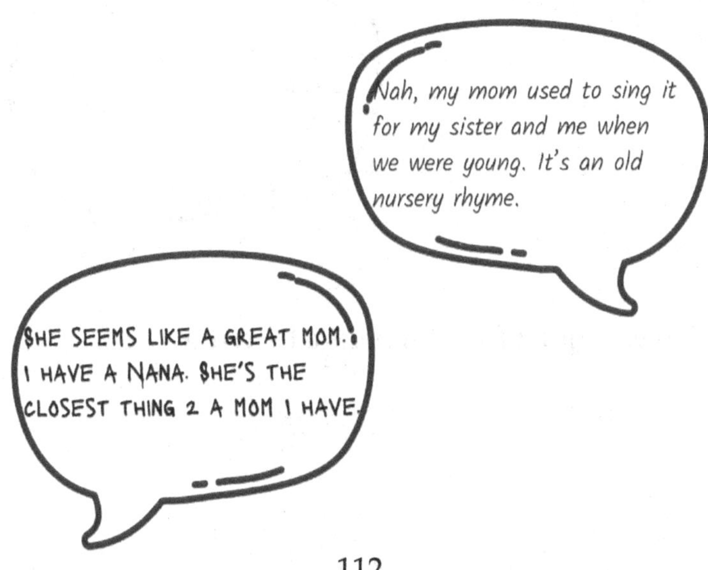

I felt sorry for him. A terrible pressure built behind my chest. How horrible must it be not to have your parent around?

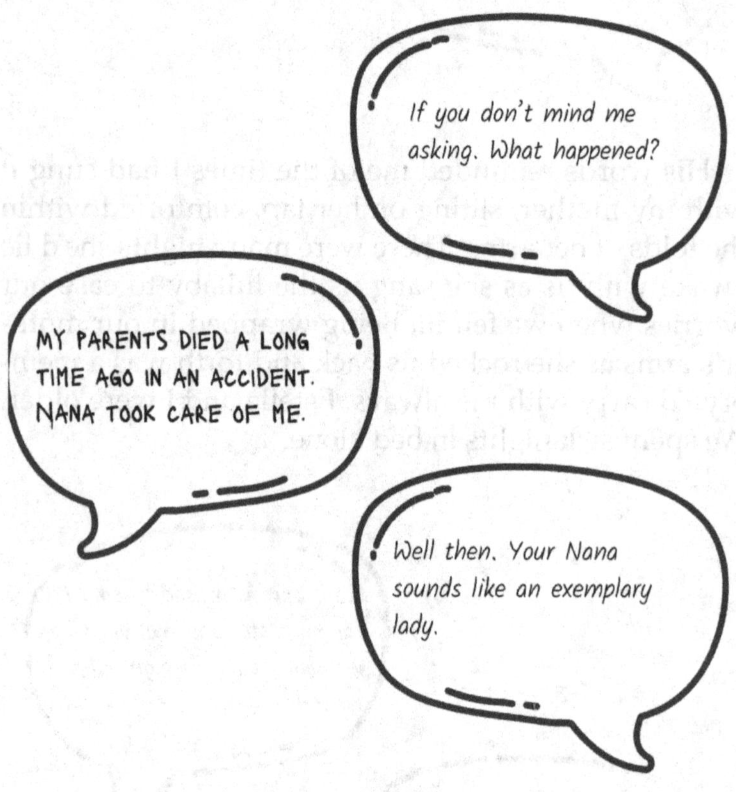

He was quiet for a bit before he wrote back.

The air in my lungs escaped. Did Marcus *really* want to meet me? I wanted to scream my joy out loud but stayed composed. Oh, who was I kidding? Marcus was not here right now to see me as I rolled back and forth on my bed with glee. Lying on my back, spread eagle on the fluffy flowery comforter, I basked in the words I read. He wanted to meet me. Maybe Marcus felt the same way I did when we texted each other. Taking a deep breath, I rolled back onto my stomach and picked up the phone. With shaky fingers, I got back to the last message he sent me. I wasn't sure I knew how to continue the conversation without sounding like a total idiot. Thinking it was better to stick with humor, I text:

He made it easy for me to smile.

Placing the phone back on the bed, I thought about Marcus and what he was doing at the moment. If my imagination was on point, Marcus would most likely be lying in bed with a plethora of soft pillows. His chest was bare and delicious. I squeezed my eyes tightly shut. A sigh escaped my lips at the thought of how a male twenty-year-old body might look on him.

I giggled at his silliness, fully oblivious to his flirting until it finally sank in.

The blush in my cheeks radiated to every part of me. My entire body went red as I appeared at a loss for words. There wasn't a manual for this kind of stuff. How was it that Marcus was so good at flirting and I sounded so naive and stupid? I took a deep breath and wrote. I didn't know how it happened, but even though I had never seen Marcus face to face, I couldn't keep enjoying our messages' progression.

Marcus was such a sweet talker. I grinned. Oh! I almost forgot to tell him about my win today. I went on to type.

Guess what? I just won…

I didn't even get to finish writing what I wanted before mom hollered for me to come downstairs and help set the table. The smell of sauce and herbs permeated the room. *Yum! Oh, well.* Marcus would have to wait until later because tonight called for a late-night order of pizza.

Dylan Marcus Taylor

I STRETCHED MY arms over my head as sunlight streamed into the hotel room. A knock sounded at the main door, pulling me out of bed. I scratched my chest as I pulled on the hotel's courtesy bathrobe, only wearing a pair of loose drawstring pants. I unlocked the door to see the hotel manager standing on the other side.

"I'm sorry to wake you, Mister Taylor, but your ride to the airport is here."

I thanked him for the notice and their hospitality and went back inside to finish packing the rest of my things. I took a twenty-second shower then threw on a pair of jeans and a sweater. Slipping on my boots, I saw my phone screen light up on the table where I had left it last night. One quick look at my watch said I was extremely late. I opened up my phone to see Bree had sent me a message, smiling to myself at the name change.

The phone in my hotel room rang again. I knew it was Robin because I wasn't answering her calls on the cell phone. I quickly wrote Bree back while yanking the charger out of the European outlets.

I ran around the room again to ensure I had everything put together when I heard another knock on the door. I called out to the valet to come inside and grab my bags. Taking another quick look around, I ran out the door behind the valet, watching as my bodyguards flanked me. Once downstairs, I waved at the manager, who took that as a check-out sign, and walked back outside into the brisk cold air. A passerby saw me and asked for my autograph in French. I signed the paper for the couple and got inside the limo that waited for me before the paparazzi showed. The driver closed the trunk after stashing my bags and got into the front. As we drove in peaceful silence to the airport, I called my irritating agent back.

I would have taken a private jet, but I didn't have one ready, so I opted to take a commercial. Except, the airport was busy. I had sat next to a man who snored up and down first class, and when I landed after a half a day's flight, I found out I had one piece of luggage missing. Calling Robin to deal with the matter, I got into the car my driver Barron had waiting for me at the airport and headed home. From there, I had to shower and change to make it to another meeting in time. At least until my cousin's event, I would be swamped for the next few days.

Too damn busy.

DESPITE HAVING A few hours of rest after such a long flight, and a day fully packed with meetings, I zoned out in the conference room chair as the meeting with my cousin and his publicists about the unveiling of Sheik droned on. I heard the guy talk about the products going into the bag, media that got invited, as well as famous magazines, and about my contract with Juniel Taylor-Lemore fragrances. He reminded me that June's cologne line is the only one I should wear to events not to cause any controversy.

As if I didn't already know that.

Not like I'd wear anything else. I was not too fond of men's cologne, preferring to wear body sprays instead, which were a lot less dense. My cousin's formula had been the only one that smelled good, and my skin could tolerate without going into hives. I heard the guy drone on, but this time I had no idea what he said because I had gone entirely under.

Jolting me awake with an elbow to the rib, June coughed to cover the sounds of what might have been a snore. "Dylan, were you sleeping?" My cousin murmured the words, so only we two could hear, but the silence in the room made it clear they caught me sleeping.

I straightened up in the highly comfortable chair, rolling my shoulders around. "Yeah, my bad. Not that you're boring" —I pointed at the publicist, who looked affronted— "but I barely got enough sleep last night, and I had just come in from a long flight the day before."

June started laughing at the shocked expression on his publicist's face. He also took a good look at me. He must've seen how worn out I felt. "Carl, let's wrap things up quickly. Is there anything else that's important you need to tell my cousin?"

The guy named Carl shook his head and cleared his throat. "Uh, no. I think that's it. Everything else is just second nature to Dylan."

I managed to smirk as I yawned behind my hand. It's always second nature. Meet, greet, schmooze… yadda yadda.

"Well then, I guess we're done. Just make sure that you prepare the extra goody bag for the winner. I want her bag to be better than the regular ones we are handing out."

Carl nodded and walked out of June's office.

Yawning again, I slumped in the chair with the back of my neck resting at the top. "I'm so damn tired!"

June shook his head. "What's up, Dy? You've only been like this once before, and that was when you were filming *Girl Up the Street* and *Love Spies* at the same time."

Jeez, reminding me of all those cheesy-ass movies made me want to hibernate in seclusion. Everyone thought my looks were perfect for romantic dramas and comedies, so I was booked repeatedly for the same roles. *God, I am so glad I got the part as the villain in a darker action flick.* I was finally going to get into the characters I wanted. Some guys enjoyed being the warm golden god of the screen, but I preferred more intriguing parts. Being a villain for once was going to be a significant catalyst for change in my filmography.

I snorted. "It's just been meetings after meetings. Usually, I get a good enough night's sleep, but I have to rub elbows with so many people right now. I need a break, June. I want a damn vacation where I don't have to worry about paparazzi and could just chill at the beach with someone. Ah, heck. I don't even know anymore."

Juniel stood up from the chair he sat in at the conference table. "It seems what you need is a long-term distraction, and I have the perfect woman for you."

One eyebrow drew up. "Francesca Petra?" I joked.

June took a bean bag from his desk and threw it at me, hitting me right smack in the back of the head. "Ouch, June. I was kidding."

"Francesca Petra is mine, but no...the girl I have in

mind seems perfect."

"Seems?"

June shrugged his pointy shoulders. "I haven't met her in person yet."

It seems that my cousin and I were more alike than we thought. I had to be Marcus to talk to one of the most genuine girls I'd ever had the pleasure to get to know, and my cousin June must have seen the very same thing in the mystery girl.

"And what makes you think she's so perfect?"

June had a mischievous smile on his face. "She is the sweetest thing—my contest winner. We spoke on the phone a few days back. Throaty voice, very sexy. She's young but seems genuine."

"Great. Win a contest, date Dylan Taylor. Hmm… It might be good publicity. I should talk to Robin about it."

June threw another beanbag, but I caught it one-handed and sent it flying right back this time. He ducked and laughed. "Quit joking around, Dy. You would never do something so corny. I happened to meet her through the contest, but you get to meet her yourself on Friday night, and you'll see exactly what I felt when I talked to her."

"So why don't you date her?"

June's smile was cheesier than cheddar. "Because I'm in love with Francesca Petra."

I snorted again. Juniel was always in love with a new model. This time it happened to be the famous supermodel Francesca Petra who agreed to be his date for the unveiling.

"I'm serious, Dy…" June began. "This girl was

sweet, smart, and so down to earth. I think she's one of those girls that will like you for you and not for what you bring to the table. You know?"

Yeah, I did know. I knew that I had met that kind of person with Bree. Would meeting this new girl mean I would be two-timing Bree? *Damn.* Why was I even thinking about it? I ran fingers through my hair in frustration. I hadn't yet met either of them in person. But, if I had a chance to meet at least one of them this Friday, without making any commitments, then I would.

Brina Palace

"SO IN CONCLUSION, Macbeth expresses one of the most important elements in Christian tragedy, and that is the fall of man…." I finished the conclusion to my essay on Shakespeare's Macbeth. The teacher gave extra credit for saying the report in front of the class, so I jumped at the opportunity for a better grade. Some students clapped while others yawned. I sat back down at my desk while another student got up to read their essay for the class. I listened to my classmate drawl about the play *A Midsummer Night's Dream* for their topic on Shakespeare that month while keeping an eye on the clock on the wall.

The time ticked by ever so slowly. The time read eleven-thirty-eight in the morning. Estella and I were leaving at noon today because of the Juniel Taylor-Lemore event tonight. I was excited and felt privileged to be a part of such a prestigious event. To think that I would meet some famous people like Juniel's date, Verogue's international model Francesca Petra. Juniel who happened to be an extraordinarily gifted entrepreneur to have his line of fragrances. Players from New England Patriots football team would be there, and of course, Dylan Taylor. I stared back up at the clock—eleven-thirty-nine in the morning.

Darn!

If I kept gawking at the time, it would end up moving backward instead of forward. I stopped thinking about tonight's event and the fact that I had hours of make-over time to go through. Instead, I focused on my classmate's lesson. There were many principal characters in the play *A Midsummer Night's Dream*, but they all seemed to center around the half-man, half-goat guy. I got so enthralled with the essay read that I didn't realize the guy sitting next to me tried several times to catch my attention. He nudged my arm with his elbow. I jerked in my seat and glanced over at him.

He didn't say anything but pointed to the classroom door. Behind the door's window, I saw my sister waving her hands, trying to grab my attention. I immediately faced forward in case the teacher caught me staring. The occupied professor was engrossed in another essay read out loud to notice anything amiss, and I was grateful for that. I stared at the door again to see a frustrated Estella. Knowing my sister would make a scene, I sighed and raised my hand, ashamed that I interrupted my classmate.

"Excuse me, Mister Charles," I called out.

The professor looked over at me with a sour expression. "Excuse me, Miss Lowell, but it seems Miss Palace needs my attention so urgently that she felt the need to interrupt you."

I paled. Mister Charles was not a teacher; anyone wanted to get upset. I honestly did feel ashamed of myself, but it had to be essential for my sister to come to my class to get my attention.

"Could I please get excused to go to the bathroom?"

He frowned.

"It's important," I added.

"Important enough that if you don't go now, I'm going to have a mess in my class later?" I paled further as students around me snickered. I deserved it.

I nodded, afraid to say anything else.

"Fine. Get on with it."

He signed over a pass, and I walked out of the classroom as quickly as my feet took me. *I don't think there is an actual day where I'm not embarrassed out of my mind,* I thought to myself. I closed the door behind me and looked around for my sister. Estella stood by the lockers in a lip-lock with her boyfriend. I took a deep breath and slowly walked over to my sister, hoping that she would finish the kiss before I got to them. The heavens were not looking out for me at the moment. I cleared my throat, annoyed I had to break them apart but took perverse satisfaction in their scared expressions.

Estella composed herself first. "Sheesh, Brina. The least you could've done is given some warning before clearing your throat like you're the school administration."

I shrugged. "Sorry, you got a little something here," I said to my sister while pointing to the side of her mouth.

Estella took her thumb to wipe at the smeared lip-stick. Her boyfriend swiped at his mouth too. She pulled out a compact and fixed herself as if nothing ever happened. Once Estella retouched her lipstick, she put her compact away.

"Whatever. Anyways, I'm just letting you know that I'm leaving right now. My stylist has to fix the high-lights in my hair, so I have to see her this instant. I can't wait for you to get out."

I couldn't believe this. "Are you serious, Estella? It's only like twenty more minutes."

Estella studied her polished fingernails. I wanted to scream.

"Just take a cab."

I was finally at a loss. Frustrated, I growled. My voice echoed in the empty walls.

Estella walked away with her boyfriend in hand, leaving me to stomp my feet like a petulant child.

"Miss Palace!"

Double darn.

I was in deep, deep trouble. My English teacher stood by the door of his classroom. The corners of his mouth were so inverted I wouldn't have thought it possible had I not seen it for myself. I walked back with my head down because I knew I was in huge trouble.

"Please get inside the classroom, Miss Palace." I slowly made my way to him as the class silently watched from their seats. "Oh, and Miss Palace?"

I turned back to Mister Charles.

"Expect to stay after school on Monday."

I had never gotten detention before. I sighed. "Yes,

sir."

Once in the classroom, I kept my face on my papers, afraid to look at anyone else. I sat quietly in my chair for the next fifteen minutes of class—the boy who had initially tried to get my attention grinned and gave me the thumbs up. I blushed, biting my lip and keeping the smile off my face. Another student had gone up to recite their essay for the remainder of the period. I still couldn't believe I got detention because of my inconsiderate sister. As soon as the time was up, the bell went off and dismissed all the classes.

Instead of heading to my next class, I walked outside and down the street where I knew a depot would be. After walking for ten minutes in the cool April air, I made it to the transport station. I knew I would be late to the hair salon if I took a bus or subway, so I walked over to the parked taxi cabs to take me downtown. I got inside a vacant car and told the driver where to go.

After about another twenty minutes in the cab, I paid the driver his fare and walked inside the beauty salon my sister, dog, and mother frequented on a routine basis.

The moment I walked in, I heard one of the stylists' yelp, "It is about time you arrived."

Startled, I responded incoherently. "Huh?"

The woman ushered me inside. "You're Brina, right?"

I blinked. "How did you know?"

The stylist whose tag said *Mary* waved her question away. "Honey, I was told to look for a wild-haired brunette with chewed-up lips and freckles."

I raised an eyebrow. It must have been my sister to

describe me as such a wild child.

"But, instead, I found a young girl who has luscious dark hair with natural body and bounce, large rosy lips, and the cutest light dusting of freckles."

It seemed my stylist Mary would be earning a substantial tip today.

SWEET LORD JESUS, they were finally done with my hair. Mary said beauty took time and patience, but I lost my composure when they untangled my hair and each minute swept away with every roller that went into my long brown locks. I couldn't remember the last time I ever saw the inside of a salon. The stylist cut my long hair in layers and styled it into loose curls and waves around my face. While I sat under the hair blower, the make-up artist the salon brought in to do my face said it was her best work yet. Staring at my reflection in the mirror, I had to agree.

The fine powder and brown liner made my eyes

pop, and the coral blush was enough to give me a permanent flush for the rest of the night. My freckles were barely visible under the powder concealer and highlighter. I wore a shiny pink gloss that emphasized my lips but did not overindulge them. The makeup artist had also slapped me on the hand twice because I chewed off her lip gloss every time I gnawed on my lips. In the end, the artist gave me the gloss and brush.

Estella had finished with her hair and make-up, so I got up from the seat in the waiting room and followed her out to her car. With fingernails and toes already done, all we had to do was go home, shower, and change into our new clothes.

Mom was so excited for us that she had taken us shopping the day before for new dresses. I did not wear dresses, but my mother was so happy I didn't want to ruin the mood. Estella's choices had been easy because everything fit great on her tall, slender frame. Being a tad thicker than Estella and a lot shorter, what looked good on Estella or the mannequin did not look good on me. Ultimately, after several wardrobe changes, we had finally settled on "the one."

Time flew as Estella and I showered, careful not to wet our hair or faces, and changed into our clothes for the night. In less than an hour, the limo would arrive to pick us up. Our mom was busy snapping pictures as if it were prom night. She worked for a famous magazine, so the event was already news, and adding photos of the lucky winner and guest, which happened to be her daughters, would surely boost her sales.

I glanced into the hallway mirror and couldn't believe the girl who looked back at me—a beauty in a white Grecian-inspired cocktail dress that fit like a second skin. The dress was strapless with a hand-painted design around the waist in gold. I walked around with strappy stiletto heels that wrapped around each ankle in gold. I felt like a princess.

Like Cinderella for one night at least.

Estella walked down the stairs like a true goddess of our time. I couldn't get over the fact that I would never measure up to her. No matter *how* pretty I thought I looked, Estella always looked better. She wore a long canary yellow evening dress, silhouette fitting, with a deep *V*-necklace in trimming and a key-hole at the end of the *V*. Her hair was long and loose in pale gold with a diamond clip on one side. She wore platform, open-toed stilettos and held a beaded clutch in one hand.

I had to take a small purse to carry my new gloss, ID, some cash, and the event tickets inside. Knowing I only had enough space for one phone, I decided to squeeze Marcus's phone into the bag instead of my own. I hoped to talk to him at some point tonight. I got to text him that I won tickets to an event, but all he responded was with a "great." We'd barely spoken to one another unless it was to say a quick hi and bye. He was busy, and I was as well, but it didn't mean that I wasn't missing his texts like crazy right now.

"Oh, look at my two girls!" our mother shrieked when she saw the final transformation. The camera came back up.

Estella and I smiled at our parents, who proudly stood on the stoop of our home. We saw the limo rounding the corner and anxiously anticipated the evening festivities.

Cinderella was finally going to the ball.

Dylan Marcus Taylor

I WAS FORTUNATE my hand hadn't already fallen off after shaking the hands of several guests congratulating me on my cousin's successful perfume line. *As if I had anything to do with it!* It didn't bother June as much as it bothered me. People gathered around June, animatedly talking his ear off about plans and ideas they had for his fragrances. I sipped my drink and took another look around the conference hall. It was massive and decorated to fit June's tastes. The event turned out to be a huge success. I stared at my phone, hoping to receive a text from Bree, but I'd gotten nothing for the past two days.

This loss was partly my fault because I was busy, but I missed talking to her. The last thing she told me was that she'd won a couple of tickets to an event in her area, and I was happy for her. I forgot to ask her what it was for or when, but it must have been too late when I remembered. Sending her the message yesterday, I had yet to hear back from her.

I smelled her before she slid to my side. "Hello, Vanessa."

"Good evening, Darling. You look dashing tonight." She giggled while placing her hand on my bicep.

I dressed in a Hugo Boss trim fit suit in black with a light blue button-down underneath the jacket and a

135

bright sapphire blue tie. My jet-black hair was slicked back and shiny like my shiny Hugo Boss vermin boots. I wore an Emporio Armani watch on one wrist and a two-toned braided leather bracelet by Gucci on the other. All designer goods given to my manager in the hopes I would represent their brand in front of millions of people. It was the only reason I knew what I wore; if not, I wouldn't have cared what label they were so long as it looked and felt good to me. Vanessa looked gorgeous as always in a long black evening dress. Her pinned-up hair had a few loose blonde curls falling over her shoulder.

"You look beautiful as well, Vanessa."

She talked about her new movie with costar Ashton Bradford when my phone vibrated. I apologized to Vanessa as I pulled my phone out of my jacket pocket to check my messages. I had two missed calls I was unaware of—both from my agent and one note from Bree. The smile I reserved only for Bree lit up my face as I read the contents.

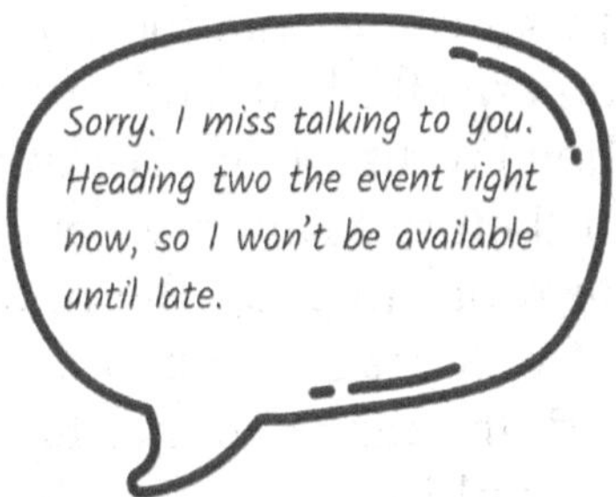

I frowned as curiosity consumed me. Where was Bree going tonight? I knew she liked premieres, but there weren't any that I was aware of in town. I decided to ask.

Vanessa laughed loudly at something June whispered in her ear. Other young ladies clung to my cousin and Francesca. The moment I put my phone back into my pocket, a plethora of women and men came to surround me too. I sighed but kept a forced smile on my face. People laughed and talked loudly to one another when an even louder uproar came from the front of the double doors where cameras flashed, and murmurs reached my ears. My phone went off, but I didn't even have time to glance at it before I saw my cousin ushered to the front of the room to greet the new guests, and his old cluster of entourage surrounded me instead. From what I heard, the ticket winner had arrived, and from my spot, I could see two females. One female was blonde in a long yellow dress, and a brunette I could barely see in a short white cocktail dress stood off to the side. They seemed familiar, but I couldn't place them.

A gentleman asked me if I planned to do the new movie overseas or in the states, startling me out of my blatant observation of the newcomers. I was accustomed to performing in romantic comedies or dramas, but never an action flick. They needed a young male to play the role of a secretly twisted international agent. He preyed on young women during the night and, by day, was a top-standing agent. Although this new role excited me, mainly because I was no longer the hero of the story but the villain, this was a new branch of my career tree. I couldn't wait to get started on the project, especially with veteran Bruce Wilson as my opposite.

"The movie will be filmed in the states as well as in Europe," I replied to the gentleman. There were only certain things I was allowed to tell the general public, so I wasn't worried about saying too much.

The crowd thinned out a little around me, so I took that quick opportunity to check my phone.

My heart dropped into the pit of my stomach with a slight ringing in my ears for added effect. The girl I had spent days obsessing over was here at the same event I was. Right here and right now. My eyebrows drew together as images formed in my head of her appearance. Would she be genuinely as gawky as she claimed or as beautiful as I imagined her to be?

"Dylan."

What if we didn't hit it off and were completely wrong for one another. Or what if Bree was a stalker and would go psycho crazy around me? *Damn!* What if she was a gold-digging hussy like Nana called them?

"Dylan."

Then there was the possibility that she was as I imagined her—beautiful, both inside and out. Smart and funny and...

"Yo, Dylan!" I heard my cousin yell.

I snapped my head up at the sound of my name. Coming face to face with June, who stood in front of me decked out in an Armani suit. His short hair gelled back exposed two diamond studs in each ear. I put the phone back into my pocket while glancing conspicuously behind June.

"I'm sorry. I must have zoned out for a second there," I uttered.

June gave me a look that told me to get it together and laughed to cover my flub while moving to the side to encompass two females—the blonde and brunette from the entrance. The blonde was lively and immediately shook my hand when June introduced us. She was gorgeous. She looked exactly like every other girl that hung on my arms in social circles. Very beautiful, but not my type. He said her name, but it barely registered.

"And this is the winner, Brina Palace."

Bree...

I knew the moment she glanced up and into my

eyes that I was smitten. I also knew where I had seen them before. At my premiere, the blonde stood to the side while her sister sat embarrassed on the floor. I remembered helping her up from the floor and getting lost in her wide green eyes. This woman was my Bree. She was the girl fate had decided to be the finder of my cell phone. The girl I couldn't stop talking to.

I offered with a wink: "It is a pleasure to meet you." She immediately blushed past the already made-up cheeks.

Her hand was soft, fitting perfectly in my palm. I fought hard with myself to let go. "Please, can I get you ladies something to drink?"

The blonde, whose name was Estella, spoke up first. "I'd just love a sparkling water."

I studied Bree, waiting for her to look at me, to say something—anything. I was dying to hear her voice after two weeks of text messages. The anticipation was killing me inside. She bit her lip and briefly glanced up at me with those big eyes blinking back at me. My entire body erupted in goose-bumps. It took everything I had not to want to touch the lip she bit. When she opened her mouth and asked for a Sprite, I thought I heard angels sing. Her voice was as I imagined, only better—way, way better.

When I stepped away from the group to get the drinks, women of all ages instantly ambushed me. While I hurried and pushed through the plethora of people, I signed autographs for some and removed roaming hands from others. Brina Palace. I couldn't believe my luck. She was standing right in front of me, only a few feet away, and she was more beautiful than

I could have ever hoped.

Grabbing the drinks, I walked back to my cousin and the two sisters. My cousin's date entertained her own crowd. I handed Brina her glass first and then the water to her sister Estella. June told them about the new perfume in his fun-loving way—keeping the girls enraptured. I made a point to stand beside Bree, who would go all stiff anytime my arm rubbed against hers. I would have laughed out loud if I didn't think it was inappropriate to do so. Trying to steal another look at her blush, I took the phone out of my pocket.

I clicked send, and seconds later, I felt the clutch she held at her side vibrate. Bree was so beautiful it amazed me she thought of herself as unattractive. *Damn!* If I'd only known before who she was, I wouldn't have wasted so much time keeping our conversations to only texts. June was minutes away from addressing the crowd gathered tonight. He excused himself to prepare, leaving Bree and Estella alone with me. Shortly after that, Estella took over the conversation like a woman used to the limelight.

"Dylan, I heard you are filming a new movie. I was

at the premiere of Breathless. It most definitely took my breath away. Fantastic movie."

I smiled as genuinely as I could. "Thank you for your patronage. I enjoyed filming Breathless. I'm glad you liked it."

Estella asked me different questions and told me more about herself. I took a peek at Bree, who surreptitiously pulled out my phone from her clutch and read the message I had sent. Like I knew she would, she blushed a bright pink. Bree sent a quick note and put the phone back in her purse. All the while, her sister yapped away, oblivious.

"So you are a cheerleader? Senior year? That's great. Cherish those years. As a matter of fact, I know someone you might like to meet." I offered Estella the crook of my elbow, all the while apologizing to Bree—assuring her I would be right back.

With Estella clinging on tightly, I walked her over to a friend on the roster as a New England cheerleader. Making the brief introductions, while June took front stage, I checked my phone as I made my way back to Bree. Estella immediately brought his friend into a conversation about their respected career choices.

I silently laughed to myself. My cousin talked about the line and what it meant to him to have such a positive turnout. He explained the history of how he got started, but I was too busy looking for Brina to care. I was stopped several times by a few people trying to grab my attention, but only one person had my undivided attention at the moment, whether she knew it or not.

Bree was the woman I had been waiting to meet.

She's exactly what I needed.

Brina Palace

SOME PEOPLE GET lucky once in their lives, but I got blessed with two extraordinary circumstances that would imprint on my mind forever. I sat down at one of the tables set up in the big hall. The tables had been decorated intricately in silver and magenta, the colors of the Sheik bottle. There were copious amounts of gorgeous women everywhere and men equally as handsome standing by their sides. I still couldn't believe that I was in this place with all of these beautiful people. How could lady luck be so generous?

I got to meet the designer of my favorite perfume and my idol crush, Dylan Taylor. My entire body had erupted into goosebumps the moment June walked us toward him. He had stared at his phone in sheer rapture as if something had absorbed him completely. Being near him, though, was short-lived. Unfortunately, precisely as I knew it would happen, Dylan had taken a liking to Estella. I watched as he guided her to a group of people standing near the bar. That is one of the reasons why I was so nervous about eventually introducing Marcus to Estella. Every guy who ever talked to me only did so to get closer to my sister. Unfortunately, they didn't account for our lack of a relationship.

I sighed.

Dylan had quickly taken her away with him, leaving me alone in a place full of strangers. It was not like he had to come back. I hadn't expected to meet both the famous cousins and spend the rest of my night with them. Wishing something like that would be greedy. I was happy to have gotten this opportunity. Juniel was the same in person as he was over the phone with me. I enjoyed his conversations. We clicked on a level that felt like family. With Dylan, I surprisingly felt like he reminded me of someone, but then I'd see him with other people and come to a conclusion once more that he was a superstar and not someone I knew.

"I'm sorry I took so long."

I almost jumped out of my seat when his voice trickled down the heightened goosebumps on my flesh. Dylan Taylor stood behind me with a saucy grin on his face. Did he come back for me? He pulled out the seat next to me and sat down. His long legs stretched endlessly under the table. He stretched out one arm and laid it on top of the back of my chair, giving me the illusion that he had his arm wrapped around my shoulders. My heart skipped a beat and then another. If I died right here, I'd die a very happy girl. His other hand lay on his lap. The strength in his hands was visible through his skin. I was stricken when my eyes made contact with his dark brown ones. Black eyelashes and thick eyebrows framed them, and his stare felt almost intimate. If I leaned back slightly, I could pretend he had his arm around my shoulders and we were more here as dates.

Instead, "Thank you" was the first thing out of my mouth.

His mouth lifted slightly on one side. "Not a problem. I did say I'd be right back."

I realized he misunderstood me, but it wasn't his fault. It was stupid of me to expect him to remember me from the premiere disaster I had experienced.

"That too, but I meant to thank you for helping me out at the premiere."

He nodded with that gorgeous smile of his plastered on his face. The smile was a lot more different than the ones he reserved for the cameras.

"I remember you, Brina." He turned to face me, flashing the full force of his smile my way.

Dylan Taylor always smiled in interviews, premieres, and around paparazzi, but it felt that it was a smile that he used habitually, not one as genuine as the one he gifted me with right now.

"And you're welcome. If anything, I should be the

one apologizing."

I was startled by his declaration. "Why is that?"

Dylan leaned in closer. He must have been unaware of the way he took my breath away if he did it so casually. "They were my crazed fans that knocked you on your butt."

I was shocked by his apology. He didn't need to apologize for something entirely out of his control. There was no way he could have stopped the overly aggressive fans at his premiere from wanting him to themselves. There wasn't one person I knew who didn't want a piece, any piece, of Dylan Taylor—myself included.

"Oh, no way. Mister Taylor, that wasn't at all your fault."

He brushed a strand of hair off of my face. The act was so innocent, yet it brought goosebumps down my entire body, from my head to the tips of my toes.

"Please, call me Dylan."

Heat flared in my face. I knew I must have turned as red as a ripe tomato. Dylan Taylor asked me to speak informally to him as if we were friends. I was in awe of this guy; it was unbelievable to have him this close. Not even because of his attraction level, even though it was somewhat high, but because of his philanthropy. He was kind to all his fans, he visited hospitals frequently to brighten the days of several sick children, and rumor mills claimed he had given away his own money for important causes. His acting was to be awarded and to top it off; he was sweet with an average girl from New Salem.

"I'll gladly call you Dylan if you call me Bree."

For a second, I noticed his eyes brighten. This time, when he smiled, he seemed like a man in love. I mentally shook my head. This weird line of fantasizing had to stop. Dylan was a seasoned actor and was only being kind to his cousin's event winner.

Either way and for whatever reason, he just radiated when he smiled and whispered, "Agreed."

I could picture Marcus with that smile. But for some reason, I could only imagine Dylan's face as Marcus. I was losing it.

We both glanced over at the stage. Juniel concluded his speech, and the crowd broke out into applause. I stood from my chair with Dylan following suit as we both clapped for Juniel and his achievements. My eyes roamed down to where my clutch sat at the table. Something was off with me. I stood in a vast room of famous entertainers, rubbing elbows with the beautiful people, but I felt incomplete.

Here Dylan Taylor stood next to me, but all I could think of was Marcus. What was he doing or who was he doing it with? I had barely spoken to him the past few days since his departure overseas, which had put a damper on my mood. It only confirmed that I was well and truly addicted to his messages. Clearing my throat, I momentarily excused myself from Dylan, who watched me with soft eyes. At least, I thought he looked at me as if he cared.

Weird.

I saw Dylan sitting at the table enveloped by females and males alike from my spot in the back. Estella laughed with another beautiful blonde and a guy who may have been a New England football player. Juniel stood beside the beautiful French supermodel Francesca Petra. As impressive as everything seemed, I knew I didn't belong here. When I fantasize about being rich or glamorous, it's a lot more desirable than this very moment. It made me realize that being glamorous only worked for me if I was with someone that made me feel ten times more beautiful. I was happy for the opportunity to be someone as beautiful as the rest, even if it was for one night. I felt the familiar vibration go off in my hand as I was about to put the phone back into my clutch.

I sure wished he was, but it was impossible to be in a relationship with someone I'd never met before, let alone met me. I was, however, afraid of allowing what little connection I did have with this man go. Audibly sighing, I put away the phone and went back to the table. Dylan glanced over at me as I approached him. His eyes softened, making my restless heart tighten. Without taking his eyes off of me, he whispered something into the ear of the woman who had taken the seat I vacated earlier. The woman pouted as she got up from the chair and moved to another. Dylan patted the chair beside him, beckoning me to sit back down next to him.

"Everything okay?"

The small crowd that had gathered around us gasped, prompting me to look up from my seat. Dylan abruptly stood up from the table. Was everything okay? I nodded and smiled. He ignored the questions directed toward him, studying my face instead. If I didn't know any better, I'd think he had feelings for me—ridiculous notion. I locked my fingers together and placed them on the surface of the table, willing my heart to relax.

What is wrong with him?

He smiled, but it seemed forced, like when he usually greeted the people around him. Maybe he regretted sitting down next to me? He leaned down to whisper in my ear. The move sent goosebumps soaring on every bit of my flesh. The feel of his breath stirring the air around me shot tingles up and down my spine.

The sensation thrilled me. The current of this connection almost took my breath away.

"I need to speak to you in private. Do me the honor?"

I nodded again, afraid that if I opened my mouth, a frog would jump out.

He put his hand out, and I tentatively placed my small hand in his big one. Gently squeezing my fingers, he pulled me from my seat, inciting a few glares from the women around us. His smile remained in place as he nodded to others greeting him while carefully pulling me to the other side of the room. I tried to keep up with his pace, but these heels were hard to walk in. I tripped on the edge of the carpet runner.

My entire body heaved to one side, but Dylan noticed and twisted his body to capture the brunt of my weight on his chest. I was plastered against Dylan Taylor's body from chest to hip with his arms wrapped tightly around me. The entire world disappeared then. I couldn't hear anything beyond our heavy breaths. We stared into each other's eyes, and for a brief moment I had the insane urge to kiss him. Our brief interlude broke when the sound of camera clicks and flashes filled the room's silence. I immediately straightened myself, and Dylan dropped his arms from my heated body.

"Oh, I'm so sorry."

Dylan glanced at the hoard of photographers and spectators. He then turned to me with one of his calculated smiles. "Are you okay?"

"I am now. Thank you for catching my fall," I muttered loud enough for the nosy people to hear.

Many of them whispered to one another. I could overhear the gossipers, saying things like, "I thought she threw herself at him."

Thank goodness.

Dylan gave the eavesdroppers a calculated glare, causing them to turn face immediately. Once we were alone again, he turned to me and gave me a genuine smile with no teeth.

He gently grabbed my chin and turned me to face him. "Bree, are you okay?" The way he said my name sounded like a caress to my soul.

I cleared my throat to speak. "Yes, I'm fine. I'm sorry." I loosened the caught heel and rolled my ankle around just in case anything dislocated. "My shoe got caught on the rug."

He looked down at my foot. "Does it hurt?"

I smiled at the concern in his voice. "Nope. See?" I rolled it around again.

Dylan looked back up into my eyes but not after feeling his eyes roam up my leg and back to my face. I shivered.

"That was my fault. I shouldn't have dragged you, but I needed to speak to you. I'm..."

I felt his concern thicken. The air around us felt heavy.

He sighed and was about to open his mouth to say something when the air around us shifted, and a strong scent of perfume wafted into our secret circle. It made me sneeze. While I apologized, Dylan smothered a laugh.

"Dylan, darling, here you are."

Gorgeous and tall, Vanessa Dallas approached us. She wore a long black gown that accentuated her pale features. This woman was the one who was supposed to be by Dylan's side. She strolled in on a cloud of strong perfume. Her own signature bottle because Juniel's could never smell this bad. Her heels seemed beyond challenging to walk in, but she still managed to walk as if she floated. It was more than I could handle.

Dylan put a hand up as if to stop Vanessa from talking. "Vanessa, I'm busy right now. Can it wait?"

She stuck her lip out and frowned. "I'm sorry, did I interrupt something?"

Vanessa finally noticed me. I could feel her daggered stare as she sized me up. If only she knew I posed no challenge.

"Oh, it's nothing important. Please, carry on," I exclaimed.

Seeing that I would most definitely not pose a threat, Vanessa continued. "Dylan, there is someone you just have to speak to. He saw our movie and wants to talk money."

Dylan groaned. "Bree, I'm sorry. We'll talk later, alright?"

I waved him away with a smile on my face. "No

worries."

Dylan walked off with Vanessa. Not sure why my heart ached as he walked away. *What does he have to talk to me about? And why did I feel so conflicted all of a sudden?* Jarred from my thoughts, I noticed Juniel approach me with his date. I shook the thoughts about Dylan, Vanessa, Marcus, and the rest of the world away to place a smile on my face as he neared.

He was all grins as he introduced his date to his prize winner and vice versa. We spoke about our phone conversation and how we both thought the host was flirting with Dylan during the show's airing. His date excused herself to talk to someone, and he smiled as she walked away. Juniel seemed intrigued by the model. He was attractive. She was attractive. And clearly, he was into her. I kept my eyes on him, noting the similarities and differences between the two cousins.

Where Dylan had long hair, Juniel's was cut short. Dylan didn't sport any earrings, but his cousin wore two in each ear. Both were tall, but Dylan was more physically fit and muscled, whereas Juniel was leaner with sharper edges. They had similar laughs and tones of voice. And while Dylan was recognized worldwide. Juniel, not so much—at least for right now. At the rate he moved, everyone will use Juniel's fragrances.

Focusing back on our conversation, I laughed at his joke. "That can't truly be a toupee?" I asked.

Juniel grinned sheepishly.

While Dylan told stories through his movies, Juniel, too, possessed the same incredible talent. He told me of his publicist and how one day he ranted in the office about scheduled meetings when he passed by too close to a loose nail in the wall. It had ripped his hair off. After a brief moment of silence, the incident sparked shocked looks then an outburst of laughter throughout the conference room, which doubled as his office. The way he told the story made it seem like I was there witnessing the moment as well.

June changed the subject as I stifled my laughter. "So, what do you think of my cousin Dylan?"

I almost dropped my clutch at the quick change of subject. "W-what do you mean?"

Although I knew I didn't answer his question, it seemed Juniel was satisfied with the answer from his Cheshire grin smile.

"Just that. What do you think of Dylan? Is he attractive, is he rich, nice…what?"

Being put on the spot stumped me, but I answered as honestly as possible, although my insides felt like gelatin. "Dylan seems very nice. A lot nicer than he is in interviews if I'm not too honest. Of course, he's attractive. I'd be lying if I said he wasn't, but the truth also remains that he is the world of the rich and beautiful."

June watched me as I spoke. Every word out of my mouth felt studied—not scrutinized.

"I, however, live in an ordinary world where the popular walk all over the weak and a girl gets detention for lying to her teacher." I shook my head, still unable to believe I got detention today because of my selfish older sister.

I shrugged, smiling all the while.

June laughed so hard some of his drink dribbled down his chin. I covered my mouth to hide my silent laughter. I extended some cocktail napkins to him while keeping him out of sight of the cameras. He laughed again, patting the napkins on his chin.

"It's been a long time since anyone told me they got detention."

I giggled. "High school sucks."

He shook his head but kept his eyes on my face the entire time. "You'd be perfect for him," he said with a straight face.

"Hmm?" I questioned, not knowing what he meant by that.

Perfect for who?

Dylan Marcus Taylor

I LOOSENED THE dreaded tie from around my neck as I walked into my brownstone. Nana had left a light on for me in the foyer and another one in the kitchen. Stomach growling, I walked toward that general direction to get something to eat. The event was a success for June, but I got so busy greeting those who would help or hinder my business that I forgot to eat. Not like it mattered. The food served at those events was so un-filling I would've needed about six plates to feel satisfied.

The best part of the night was getting to see Bree. She was the one person I couldn't get out of my head. Beautiful, bright, and incredibly sweet. If over messages I wasn't clear enough, I hoped I had conveyed my interest in person. The problem remained that I couldn't tell her the truth about my highly close relation with Marcus.

If I did tell her something, would she have gotten mad at me for misleading her?

Worries aside, I snorted when I opened the fridge and saw an already-made sandwich and a juice bottle beside it. Nana was pretty accustomed to my late-night food binges. I grabbed the food and closed the door. As I passed the clean, quiet kitchen with its pearl white shaker cabinets and black marble countertops, I imagined seeing Brina Palace sitting with me at the long island, eating the food Nana made us.

Imagining her didn't convey precisely how beautiful she was in person. She was sweet and funny, bright and adorable. I was bothered that I couldn't spend more time with her. I had left with Vanessa to meet an investor about a new movie deal with us as leads again, but the conversation took longer than I expected.

June did me the favor and kept her company, but it didn't feel like enough. Not like it cost June much to speak to her. She was pleasant company to keep around, and every time I looked over, I could see her joyful laughter with my cousin about one subject or another. It also annoyed me that she was so much more comfortable with June than she was around me. I could even admit to being a tad bit jealous.

Some fancy, light supper was served immediately after my conversation with the investors, and my seat took me farther away from her. At the end of the night, my cousin and I bid the two sisters good night. We closed the door to the limo and watched them drive off back home.

I took one last glance at my empty kitchen and walked up to my room. Once inside my bedroom, I took off my clothes and threw them on the desk. I quickly jumped into the shower to wash off Vanessa's strong perfume, then slipped on some boxers and climbed onto the bed with my food. I put the phone on the charger and saw that I had a missed text. Grinning like a fool at the thought that it might be Bree, I clicked on the message.

Earlier in the evening, I had texted her as Marcus to make sure she had arrived home safely. When she replied that she had and would be heading straight to bed, I didn't expect to speak to her again that night. I glanced over at the clock. Or rather, so early this morning.

I took a bite of my sandwich and washed it down with some juice.

I joked.

She teased back.

My laughter filled the quiet room. Brina sounded exactly like Vanessa.

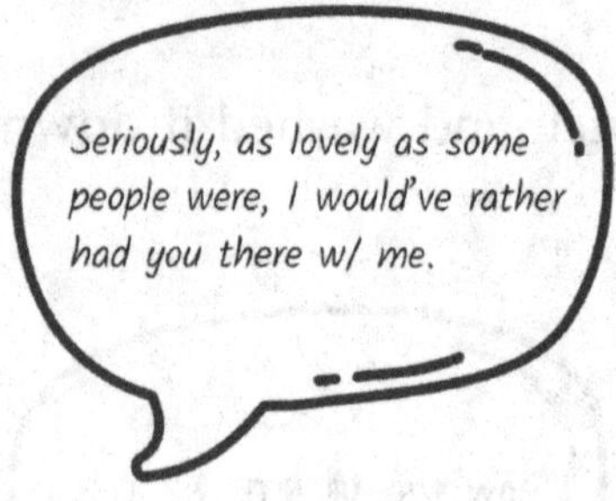

I may have been there, but I wasn't with her, and for that, I felt ashamed.

It was silent for a while before my phone went off again.

Corny? Corny was the look I had on my face at the moment. My smiled immediately faded as I searched my room for hidden cameras out of habit. For a brief moment, I forgot I was home and not Dylan Taylor, superstar. I grinned like a fool at her short declaration. She was a hell of a lot more courageous than me. That was something about Bree I never felt from anyone else in my circle. Even June got caught up in the luxury of our careers. Being around her, knowing her, made being a regular person something I truly missed. Her genuine attitude on life was something I couldn't part with.

I should've told Bree the truth today.

Now it felt like it was too late. But I didn't want to lose her. I couldn't let her go.

Dear God, I hoped she was smiling right now. By now I could've reset my password and found out where she resided, but I couldn't bring myself to break the illusion of our normal "abnormal" relationship.

My heart froze. Who could Bree's crush be? Did he meet her before the event or during it? Did he start liking her now because she dressed to kill, or did he always appreciate her?

Fingers trembling, I asked,

If it was possible to be jealous of one's self, then I most certainly was. I felt the remnants of my sandwich lodge in my throat. I should tell her the truth right now, but I couldn't get my fingers to cooperate. Instead, I asked her,

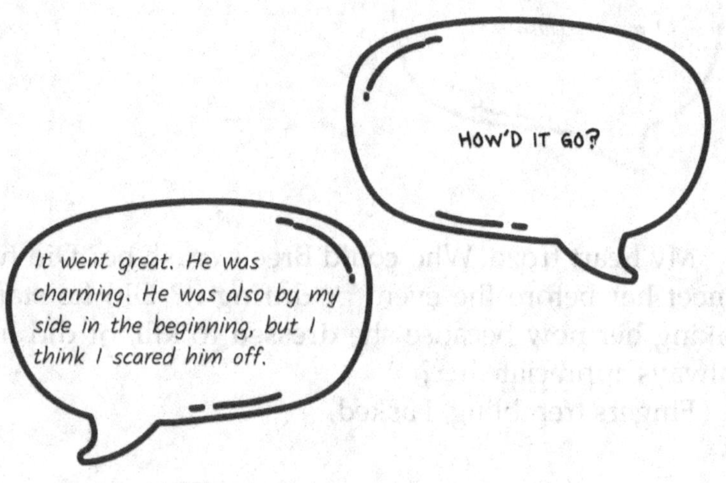

I frowned. That was so far off she'd be on the moon.

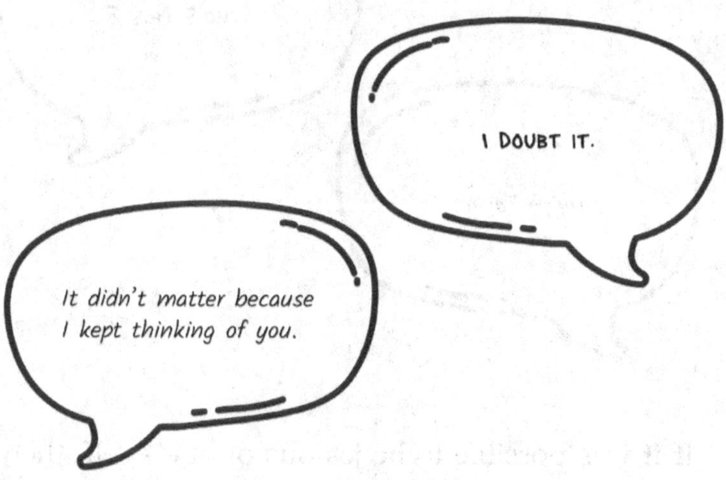

A smile remained fixed on my face. She liked me. Brina wasn't interested in Dylan Taylor. She was interested in the man I hid from the world. I needed to tell Brina the truth. So, forcing my fingers to type out the words, an incoming message lit up the screen, making me stop. I clicked on the message, automatically saving my draft.

I wanted to stop her and tell her the truth, but I'd have to wait to tell her again.

I squeezed the phone tightly in the palm of my hand as rage coursed through me, coupled with fear. No matter what excuse I came up with, I was a coward. Brina needed to know the truth, but I couldn't get myself to tell her. She meant a lot to me. Losing her now would be the biggest mistake of my life. Bree needed to fall for Dylan. Not just Marcus. She had to see us both because I was both guys—Dylan to the public and Marcus at home.

Making a decision right then, I vowed to have her know and care for both.

Brina Palace

SATURDAY WENT BY super-fast for me. My parents went off to work that morning but left a list of chores for us to take care of before they got home. I got started as soon as I woke up and tackled everything on my portion of the list. I finished some work for school and spent the rest of it talking to Marcus via message. Now with Sunday here and school the day after, I was going to spend it carefree. Marcus wrote me a lot more frequently, and I couldn't get enough of it. Our relationship got stronger after I confessed my feelings. Marcus told me he worked today on several projects, so he wouldn't be able to write me throughout the day, but that he'd message me before bed. It felt as if we were secretly dating or something similar.

It made me feel giddy.

Grabbing a pair of jeans and a soft, loose t-shirt, I got dressed and headed outside to the beautiful mid-

April air. We didn't live far from town, so I enjoyed walking there as often as possible on beautiful days like this one.

I would have taken a bike ride to cut through the woods, but my bicycle was currently out of commission, and I refused to let my parents pay for another one. Not like it worried me much. I enjoyed walking, and I loved feeling that brisk breeze on my face. Swift footsteps down the cobbled sidewalk took me past Old Man Tucker's Hardware Store. Farther down the road, my gaze spotted Mr. Beaumont's Barber Shop, where he swept the entrance of his shop. Once there, I crossed the street and waved at Sue from the bakery across the way. Her shop packed full of townies trying to get their evening desserts.

Her bakery had way too many goodies. The aroma of fresh blueberry muffins made my mouth water. There were full displays with scones, assorted cakes, and chewy-fudge brownies. Tarts of all varieties adorned one shelf, while another was full of Crème Brulee and Spanish custards. The aroma was one June needed to bottle. I walked a little farther, passing the deli and convenience store, and turned down New Salem Avenue. The old Salem Theater, which I frequented regularly, greeted me with fading red paint and buttery popcorn scent. I randomly chose a movie and walked inside.

HAVING FINISHED THE movie, I walked back outside and into the starlit night. I passed a few couples touring the small town shops hand in hand. Images of walking these streets with Marcus filled me with a warmth I couldn't describe. I bit my lip to push past the hormonal shift. I was so absorbed with phantom dates that I stopped short of hitting the street post. Reba's Antiques lit up the sidewalk. Inside the store, resting on one of the mannequins, was the most beautiful dress I had ever seen. Dresses weren't even something I wore. But somehow, I couldn't help being drawn to it. It was a lot more classic than the modern cocktail dress I had worn to the event on Friday.

I took two steps backward to get a better view of the dress. It was long and flowy. The straps seemed as if they were spun in gold, matching perfectly with the overall antique gold color of the dress. Pearl-tinted maple leaves patterned the top of the dress and swirled around the dress's bodice and down toward the bottom. Golden white stitches decorated the bottom of the dress, giving it the feel of webbing. The top of the dress was not cut into a typical straight line, nor did it have a sweetheart neckline. Its neckline instead was cut at a right angle. It was gorgeous. Afraid I would miss out on such a beautiful dress, I walked into the shop to look closer. There were dresses everywhere, but this one stood out amongst the rest.

"I see you found Mable."

The rough voice that came from behind me made me jump in my skin. The store's owner, Reba, stood before me in her funky, retro polka-dot dress and the big-hair Jersey girls were famous for. She held a small clipboard in one hand with her head tilted to the side in curiosity.

I took a cautious step back, afraid I had misstepped somehow. "Who's Mable?"

Reba pointed her pen at the dress I drooled over earlier. "She's Mable."

I knew my face had turned quizzical. "You named the dress?"

The owner smiled, exposing the crow's feet hidden under layers of make-up. She walked up to the dress she so affectionately named Mable and with wrinkled fingers stroked the patterned leaves. "Mable was owned by a 1930's lady named Mable Constance Bjork who wore the dress to a masquerade and came out of there with the love of her life, Frederick Juniper Revere," Reba explained in a voice worn from smoking too many cigarettes.

"You mean local town hero F.J. Revere. The one who singlehandedly saved the town's residents by using his farm and ranch to keep them fed and employed during the Great Depression."

Reba smiled. "You seem to know some of your town histories. Mable was F.J.'s wife, and in 1932 they gave birth to a daughter—"

"Celeste Revere, who later married the one man she thought would never give her the time of day, Mayor Gordon Blanchette," I added.

"Correct. Celeste, too, wore this dress to a function held at the mayor's house, and he was instantly smitten."

I studied the dress that had gone through so much history. To me, it did seem to be a dress with powers of love and luck. I wanted it so much for myself. Hidden under some lace was the price tag for Mable.

I blanched when I saw the price. There was no way I could ever afford this beautiful dress, even if I saved up my allowance for three years.

"She's expensive, isn't she?" Reba questioned.

I felt my stomach tie in knots. My mother would never cough up that much money for a used dress because she was more of a modern corporate woman, not classic vintage.

"I'm sure the dress is priceless, but yes, I cannot afford such a beautiful piece."

Reba smacked her lips together. "Let me ask you something, sweetheart. How did you come to see Mable in the first place?"

Her question caught me off-guard. I searched around to see that Reba had Mable tucked in the back of the store with several other mannequins dressed in even more flamboyant outfits near the corner of the end as if on display. Never to be worn, never to be touched because of its timeless feel.

"I was walking by your store and happen to see her, but she was alone. Weird, but the dress caught my attention as if displayed in the front window."

Reba smiled. "Not weird at all, dear. I bought Mable off of an estate auction and paid great money for her because she spoke to me."

I giggled. "Spoke to you, huh. I guess Mable kind of spoke to me too." I shrugged as if stating we were both going nuts.

Reba shook her head. "No, dear. The dress knows who it should belong to, and I think you're it."

"M-me?"

Reba removed Mable from the mannequin. "I'll cut

you a deal, doll. If Mable fits your body perfectly, then you could have her for whatever you have in your pocket right now as well as helping out around the shop every once in a while."

I couldn't believe my ears. Reba must be going insane if she planned on selling Mable for sixty-two dollars and forty-three cents. Besides, it didn't look like the dress would even fit me. My large hips and non-existent cleavage would never cooperate. Women back then didn't have all the curves we modern foodie women have now. Reba handed Mable over and pointed me in the direction of the fitting rooms with a quaking finger.

My heart hammered loudly in my chest, but I went on in anyway. After taking off my jeans and shirt, I pulled Mable down and over my head to let it softly slide down my chest, waist, and then hips. Mable molded me as if we were one. As I buttoned it up on the sides, I couldn't comprehend how a dress with so much history could be for me. The measurements were spot on without any alteration to be made. I couldn't believe my eyes, and I saw it for myself.

"Come on out, doll. Let me take a look," Reba cackled from behind the curtained room.

I opened the shade and stepped out, careful to hold the bottom of the dress so I didn't step on it. I spun around in front of Reba, who stood transfixed. "Well, well, sweetheart. It seems Mable has picked out her next owner."

I smiled wide. "I only have chump change compared to her price, Reba. I couldn't take her from you. I promise to come by and help as much as you'd like."

Reba waved my worries away. "Dearie, Mable chose you. I'm way too old to be fighting possessed dresses."

Our laughter filled the empty store.

Reba was far too kind and just a tad bit eccentric.

FOR SOMEONE WHO never had detention before, I didn't seem to mind it one bit, but for the fact that we got nothing done at all worthwhile. The time spent here was aggravating to say the least. The teacher in charge made us write sentences as if we were little kids the entire detention period. I didn't get to read or do homework. I had never spent my time so need-lessly, but it was far better than what I had imagined. The teacher called out that we were "dismissed," so I grabbed my bag off the floor as fast as I could and stepped out of the classroom. I got as far as a few feet before a student ran into me, slamming me hard into

174

the lockers.

An explosion burst behind my eyes when my head hit the handle of the metal locker. The instant shot of pain radiated from the inside of my skull to the tips of my toes. There were spots in my vision. Blinking, I could only focus on the blood left behind on the locker. Bile rose. Then everything spun faster than a carousel at a carnival. Students around me gathered, but I couldn't make them out. One person got closer with a hand out to steady me. I couldn't focus on who it was. Warm liquid ran down the side of my face as the world I knew went dark.

A long while later, I awoke to find I was in the Boston Children's Hospital. The nearest hospital to where we lived was the Salem Hospital, an affiliate of Mass General Brigham, so I was surprised to find myself in the massive concrete and tile palace. Although Salem Hospital was up-to-date on all the technology needed, this place was even more advanced. I turned to the side and grimaced when I felt sharp pain radiate throughout my entire body. Loads of machines annoyingly beeped away. The television was on with the volume low.

"Ugh, my head is killing me."

"Brina, baby, you fully awake?" I heard my concerned father ask.

I slowly shifted my body to see dad sitting at a small round table. He had his laptop out and paperwork scattered all over the small surface. The little corner resembled his office.

I tried to sit up. An electrifying pain jolted me back into the bed. I hissed, holding my hand gently to my head.

"Don't move, baby, don't move. You have a brain injury."

My body visibly shook. "A what?"

"It's not as bad as it sounds, but you have a concussion and had a slight hematoma that they had to drain. From what we heard, a student knocked into you pretty hard after school a few days ago."

A few days ago?

"I've been asleep for days?"

"The momentum slammed your head into one of the handles on the locker. The students who saw said that you were conscious for a few seconds before blood poured from your head. Then you collapsed."

My father cried. Tears were rushing down his face. "I'm going to go get your doctor."

I've never seen my dad look so scared before. Just then, a pale Estella walked into the hospital room with dark bruising under her eyes. She saw me sitting up on the bed and broke out into a big watery smile. My big sister came over to the bed and sat on the vacant chair beside it to hold my hand. I saw the look in my older sister's eyes and teared up myself.

"I'm fine, Estella."

Estella burst into tears. "Oh my god, Brina. It was so scary. I fight with you all the time, wishing I was an only child, but when I heard you were flown into the hospital…I almost died. It was so scary to think… to think…" She didn't get to finish the sentence when she burst into another round of tears.

I awkwardly patted her hand because of the butterfly needle embedded in my skin. Shushing sounds were all I could muster to calm my sister down. "I'm okay, Estella. That's all that matters, right?"

She nodded with jerky movements. A couple of seconds later, the door opened to reveal an older gentleman in a white coat, followed by my father and a wild-eyed mother.

"Brina, how are you feeling?" I turned to the doctor.

My nose wrinkled. "Like I was hit with a five hundred pound mallet in the head."

The doctor grinned. "Close enough. Definitely not a wooden one, though. I'd likely say it was steel."

I grinned at the crazy old doctor's response.

My mother clucked, "I do not find this situation at all hilarious."

My eyes moved to study my pale, scared mother. A woman who was a powerhouse every day, reduced to an actual fragile person. Dad came over to put an arm around his shaking wife. I felt terrible for the poor doctor who had to endure my parents' wrath this entire time.

"My apologies, Mrs. Palace, but to have Brina's humor intact is a positive sign nothing seems permanently damaged. May I proceed, Miss Palace?" he asked me.

I nodded.

From that moment on, the doctor asked me several questions, checked my vitals and retinas. He moved my limbs around and asked me to move them too. He assured us that being placed in a two-day coma was not at all uncommon for a head injury. They performed an immediate burr hole surgery to get the hematoma decompressed and drained. The surgery was successful, and they did not foresee any future problems. He explained that short-term memory loss and migraines was expected, but if I remembered the accident, there was a good chance that part wouldn't change much. Other than the few odd stitches in my head and the slight dilation in my eyes, I would be alright. At least, I hoped so. I don't think I could deal with migraines for the rest of my life.

After several hours of bad hospital food and assurances that I was alright, my mother and father had finally gone home to sleep, leaving Estella to watch over me tonight. Estella had gone home first to get extra clothes, essentials, and *real* food from our town deli. Now that she was back and we were eating our grinders in peace, I asked if my book bag was around.

"You are on a mandatory break from school, Bree. Chill out and forget about class for a bit," Estella warned.

I sighed. "I know, Estella. I just need to look for something."

Estella's pencil-thin eyebrow reached the tip of her hairline. "You mean this?" She pulled out a familiar silver phone from her back pocket.

I went pale.

"Don't worry. I didn't tell mom and dad, and I didn't go through it."

I was so surprised it showed on my face. Estella pursed her lips and smirked. "I figured it belongs to a boyfriend or something, and that's gossip I'd like to hear."

I smiled at my sister's teasing tones. It was nice to have back the older sister I used to play with when I was younger. "It does belong to a guy, but he kinda misplaced it, and so when I found it, I tried to give it back. But he said he'd rather I keep it right now so we could text each other."

Estella nodded, "He must be loaded to have such a high-tech phone." She shrugged. "That or he's deep in debt."

I didn't even think about that.

"Does he not have your cellphone number? Why does he only contact you here?"

Valid question. I answered it the best I could. "I never really got around to giving it to him. I barely used my own phone and lose it all the time."

Estella shrugged. "Makes sense. Go ahead and write him. I saw this adorable guy sitting in the cafeteria downstairs. I'm going to see if he's still there." She winked and walked to the door while wiping crumbs off her face. "You'll be okay on your own for a little?"

I nodded. "Thanks, Estella."

She waved me away and closed the door.

I couldn't believe the one-eighty my sister made at the thought of losing me. Other than the pain in my head, I didn't feel any different. I remembered the accident, but the before was a little fuzzy. My thoughts conjured up glimpses of studying and homework, but it wasn't until my parents told me I was there for detention that it came to mind.

Someone had turned off the tiny silver phone. Turning it back on, I waited until the telephone completely loaded—anxiously waiting for it to alert me of any missed messages. A couple of minutes later, the phone beeped several times. I stared at the six texts unread from Marcus.

I opened up the earliest one first, reading:

If only he knew how much I did too. I opened up the next one.

Oh, how I'd love to do just that. Runaway with him to an uninhabited beach island where only the two of us could relax and be alone together.

The following message came in at around five o'clock yesterday morning. If I remember correctly, my family told me I had come out of surgery at that time.

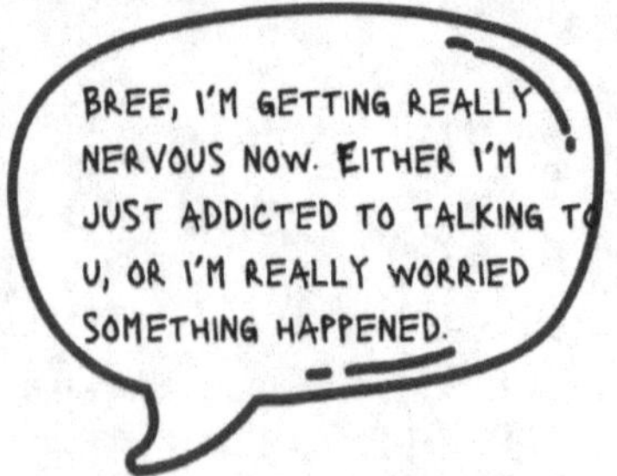

I felt like writing him back, but I had to read the rest of the messages first. Tears slowly streamed down my face. It wasn't just my imagination. Marcus did care about me.

The last one was the one that indeed broke my heart.

There was no ignoring the flutters in my stomach at the mere thought of him dashing into my hospital room like a knight in shining armor. The clock display on the phone read three minutes to eight. I quickly started typing.

I clicked send and didn't wait long before I got two responses back.

I smiled at the concern.

My heart tightened, so I placed a hand there, willing it to relax. As much as I wanted to see Marcus, I couldn't let our first time be in a hospital room, with one side of my hair partly shaved off, and in a run-of-the-mill hospital gown that let the breeze constantly through to parts better left unseen.

I bit the bottom of my lip.

There were only a few brief minutes of silence before the phone went off again.

I turned off the phone to save the rest of the battery and nestled back into the hospital bed. Marcus was so kind to me. He wanted us to meet, but I wasn't sure if I refused his visit because I was in the hospital or because I was afraid he'd take one look at me and go running for the hills.

Oh, well.

I wouldn't worry about this now. Fatigue consumed me, and my eyes fluttered shut. Tomorrow I'd think deeper on it.

Tomorrow's another day.

Dylan Marcus Taylor

EARLY THE FOLLOWING day, it didn't bother me one bit that I was heading toward the hospital to see Brina—even after she had so adamantly refused to let me come. Flying from my L.A. home that night, I got to Logan International around midnight, avoiding the flurry of daily travelers. I had woken up early to make a call to my usual florist about sending a few pieces to Brina's hospital room at Boston Children's Hospital. Signing them with an *M*, I made sure that the florists kept me anonymous to any inquiries. If anyone found out Dylan Taylor sent a teenage girl from New Salem flowers, the vultures would never leave her alone.

The first thing I did was cancel all my meetings and events with Robin. I refused to go without seeing her—even if it was under the guise of superstar Dylan Taylor. Pushing through the back doors of Boston Children's with my bodyguards, the staff took us through the usual unused stairways of the hospital. Coming to Boston Children's Hospital was also an excellent opportunity to meet my young friends in the Burn Unit. The unit's director greeted me at the door.

"Mr. Taylor, welcome back."

I shook his extended hand. "Hello again. I hope all is well."

The old, unshaved man nodded several times before speaking again. "Yes, yes. I have also prepped the parents and staff inside."

He didn't have to do that, but I appreciated it nonetheless. I only wanted to visit the children, not jeopardize my time spent with them by outrageous adults. The director opened the double doors with his ID card and let me inside. The children were playing inside a large playroom. The moment they saw me, the majority ran toward me with cheers and giggles. The little ones in this ward were severely burned and could not leave until their wounds adequately healed. I sat cross-legged on the floor, bombarded with hug after hug from these wonderfully courageous children.

"Man, I missed you guys! Look how big you've gotten," I said to one of the burn unit's residents who sat on my knee. "What are they feeding you in this place?"

Some of these children would never be able to live a healthy life again, but that didn't change the fact that they were children who still needed someone to remind them that they would be fine. They ranged from four to twelve years old and had burns from fires to actual acid assaults. Some were victims of a fire, and others were victims of parental abuse. I cared for these kids and visited them often.

"Hospital food stinks!" yelled one of the frowning little boys as he kneeled on a small futon.

He made me grin. "That's why I brought you these." I turned to gesture toward the door of the large room, and the entire league of waiters making their way inside.

They had platters of mini sandwiches, cookies, brownies, and all sorts of snacks displayed in an array of bright colors—all doctor approved. Not like it was an easy thing to do. I spent the majority of the morning getting all the last minute details out of the way and an entire plane ride with my manager getting approvals from the doctors and hospital directors. Some of the parents in the room with their kids smiled and thanked me for my generosity. All of the last minute planning was worth it. Not because I wanted to see Bree, but because I enjoyed visiting these little rascals.

I stayed around for another hour with the kids, playing games like duck, duck, goose and Simon says. I had an animal balloon artist come in to make the kids fun balloon animals and swords. Some of the little girls opted for crowns. Afterward, I waved goodbye to my buddies in the Children's Hospital Trauma and Burn Center and walked toward the elevator bank.

Bree was on a different floor for recovery, and because I knew the nurses on that floor had the best coffee, I made that my excuse for going. I got into the elevator, surprised to see a familiar blonde standing next to me with a container full of food, two sodas under her arm, a bag of chips, and a bag of snack cakes in her mouth.

The view was quite amusing.

Briefly lifting the ball cap I used to cover my hair and face, I bent low beside her. "I believe we've met before."

She looked over at me and then at the two huge bodyguards behind me, and her eyes grew as big as saucers.

"Here, let me help you." I took the sodas from her and the snack cake bag from her mouth.

"Oh my god, Dylan Taylor?" She studied the empty interior and lowered her voice. Although there was nobody else in the interior, she saddled up closer to me as if to whisper, "What are you doing here?"

A person who asked me what I was doing in a hospital because they did not know of my charity work was usually the type of person I tried to stay away from. Except, this was Bree's older sister Estella, and it was the perfect excuse to see Brina.

"I came to see some friends."

She stood quietly for a second while the elevator slowly crawled to our floor.

"We were near the Burn Unit. Your friends got burned?"

I nodded, not saying anything else.

The elevator finally stopped, dinging its arrival. Like a gentleman, the doors opened, and I let Estella walk out first, lowering the hat back down over my eyes.

"So why are *you* here?" I asked her.

"My little sister got hurt and is currently in recovery." She stared back at me as she whipped her hair to one side. Estella was indeed a remarkable-looking woman but still couldn't compare to my Brina.

I frowned. "Your sister Brina is in the hospital? Is she okay?" I needed to play the role of oblivious superstar.

She smiled at him. "Yes, she's alright. You have no idea how scary it was at first. One minute she's my annoying little sister, and the next, she's in and out of consciousness and could die at any point." Tears had slowly built in her eyes, and I saw her sincerity. No one was that good of an actor—not even me.

"I'm sorry. The best part is that Brina is alright."

She nodded and stopped when she reached the door to Bree's room. She signaled me to wait for a moment, and I did. Looking around, I saw the nurses stop to smile at me and wave a coffee around as a signal to get some. I smiled back at them and asked them to give me a few minutes. I heard Estella call out that it was safe for me to come inside, so I did.

I walked into the room and immediately searched for Brina. She was sitting up in bed with a bandage wrapped around her head. There were tiny drops of blood seeping through the dressing on one side, but it seemed controlled. Her gorgeous emerald-green eyes grew rounder when she recognized who I was. Small hands clenched the sterile white sheets on her bed, and her beautiful thick lips hung slightly open from their shock. I saw that her entire room was full of different flowers and get well balloons. Sitting at one of the roundtables, I saw a woman who looked like an older version of the two siblings. Knowing respect from my routinely disciplined bouts with Nana, I greeted the older person in the room first.

"Good morning. You must be Mrs. Palace? I'm Dylan Taylor." The woman, still in shock, shook from her state and clasped her hand with mine. We shook hands and let go at the same time.

"Yes, I am. My daughters tell me loads about you, Mister Taylor," she replied.

"Mom!" I heard come out of Estella.

I laughed as I turned to face my beautiful Bree. "Brina, how are you?"

She visibly swallowed. "I'm fine now, Mister Taylor."

I frowned. "We've gone through this, right? Please, call me Dylan."

She smirked. "Only if you call me Bree."

Laughter bubbled up inside me as I saw the error in my ways. I should've called her Bree from the very beginning. Sitting in an empty chair next to her bed, she explained what happened at school and how she ended up here. I seethed internally but dared not show my irritation toward the guy who could be so clumsy. We sat and chatted for a few minutes before we were interrupted by the girl's mother.

"Dylan, would you mind taking a picture with my daughter?"

I didn't mind it at all, but I was sure Brina would. "Mom!" she called out.

"I don't mind, so long as Bree doesn't either," I replied. My eyes were still on the brunette.

Brina had stared death at her mother, who looked unperturbed by such scrutiny. She then turned to me and smiled as she shrugged her shoulders.

"I don't mind."

I snickered as I got up from my chair. When I approached Bree's bed, I wrapped my left arm around the top. I got close to her cheek and lightly brushed against it. She must have gone bright red because I could feel the heat radiating from it. Both of us were smiling. Brina's mother snapped picture after picture of the two of us.

Estella jumped in as well and took pictures with us.

We laughed at the last one her mother snapped. I stuck my tongue out and crossed my eyes, Bree made a fish face, and Estella also crossed her eyes and gave a huge toothy grin. Not very many people enjoyed being so silly for the cameras. The moment helped remind me that they were not like the other females I was used to being around.

I got up when my phone went off. Excusing myself, I walked to the other end of the room to answer the call. My agent screamed. I pulled the phone away from my ear as she rambled on about a modeling shoot. Knowing my time with Bree was over, I walked over to her to say my goodbye properly. I shook hands with Estella and their mother, Emma, and walked over to Bree.

My heart stirred as I stared into Bree's eyes, so I leaned down and kissed her on the cheek as both Dylan and Marcus. If only she knew I was Dylan Marcus Taylor, the guy she liked and who liked her right back.

I'm a fucking igit.

"I'M IN LOVE with you, Shannon."

I watched Dylan confess his feelings to Shannon, and I got jealous. He walked over to her and wrapped his muscular arms around her tiny waist. Shannon wore a pencil skirt and maroon blouse. Her pinned-up hair bun had a pencil stuck through it. Shannon was a librarian in a little library in a town Dylan had gotten stuck in.

She burst into tears, clinging to his jacket. Then she met Dylan's eyes with her entire heart written all over her face. They appeared perfect together. I felt another stir of jealousy.

"I love you too, Daniel," she replied.

I clicked the power button on my television's remote. Why was I getting into a hissy fit watching Dylan Taylor in one of his popular romantic dramas? Why did I feel so conflicted? I talked to Marcus every single day and grew to like him more and more. Heck, it was safe to say that I was most definitely falling in love with a ghost. I'd be devastated if I ever found out Marcus was some crazy guy that had been lying to me. Now, I imagined myself with Dylan Taylor, and that was beyond stupid.

Ignoring my frustrations, I walked over to the desk to read through the finished yearbook. I was supposed to do all the last-minute editing and then send an all-clear to the manufacturing company. I only found a couple of spelling mistakes in the yearbook, so I jotted them down and put them to the side. The only thing the yearbook needed was the Prom photos. There was only a week left until Prom, and it made me melancholy at the thought. I should be happy that juniors could attend Prom, but I didn't want to go. Unfortunately, I needed to go because of the necessary pictures for the yearbook, but going alone would be humiliating.

It took three weeks to recover in the hospital. I was only allowed to walk around the hospital grounds and nowhere else where staff couldn't keep an eye on me in case I suffered any debilitating issues after the surgery. Bright lights bothered me and I was discouraged from being on the phone in the dark, but I couldn't help it. Marcus wrote me regularly, but he had been a little bit more reserved. I had finally gotten the courage to have him visit me at the hospital, but he always made excuses that he couldn't. Dylan came by again, though, with his cousin Juniel to see me.

They had stayed with me for an hour, laughing as if we were old friends all along. Now I was back home and back in school and had feelings for not just one guy, but two. What I hated was that both were out of reach. It was just like me to fall for someone I couldn't have.

There was a knock on my door, so I got up to open it. On the other side was Estella, with a beautiful ball gown in her hand.

"Mom bought me this dress for Prom. Wanna see?"

I was delighted. Estella and I had been getting along

well since the accident. My sister laid the dress out on the bed and unzipped it from the clear bag, where she safely tucked it inside. The dress was gorgeous. The beautiful gown was another yellow concoction, but this time it had swirls of purple, green, red, and blues on the bottom. It had a sweetheart neckline that shimmered in gold.

I ran my hand down the delicate dress. "Oh, Estella. It's a fabulous dress!"

Estella clapped her hands together and hugged me from the side. "I know, right?"

We talked a little more about Estella's dress as she zipped the dress inside the garment bag. As Estella walked back out of my room, she stopped and peered inside my open closet. Inside, hung my antique dress, Mable. Estella didn't even wait for clearance. She walked toward the closet and pulled the dress that had been hanging on one end. Shocked, she focused on me.

"What's this?"

She pulled the dress out of the bag Reba had placed over it and smiled. "Brina, this is beautiful. Is it your dress for Prom?"

I shrugged my shoulders. "I don't know if I want to go, Estella."

Estella whipped her head to the side to face me. "Why not? Because you don't have a date?"

I shrugged again as I gnawed on my lower lip. "I just don't fit in with that crowd, sis."

My sister put the dress down gently and hugged me. "Brina, you should go, and you should invite mystery man as your date."

I jumped at the thought of Marcus. Invite Marcus as

my date to the dance? Would he do it? If I had Marcus there, then I wouldn't feel so left out. An older guy as my date, and as successful as him, I wouldn't have to worry about getting picked on by the rest of the idiots at the dance.

Thinking of using Marcus in that way made me nauseous.

Things may have changed with my sister, but they weren't much more different at all in school. The only guy who didn't bug me was Guy Perkins, the footballer who had bumped me into the lockers. He had gotten to defending me whenever the other football players or cheerleaders gave me a hard time. He felt guilty for roughhousing with his friends in the hall after football practice and had visited me in the hospital a couple of times to make sure I was better.

My sister wrapped Mable back up into the bag and hung her in the closet. "Think about it, Bree." She placed a brief sympathetic hand on my shoulder before she walked out of my room.

Maybe my sister was right, and I should go to the dance feeling confident for once in my life. Feeling a jolt of courage, I walked over to the cell phone that belonged to him and sent a text.

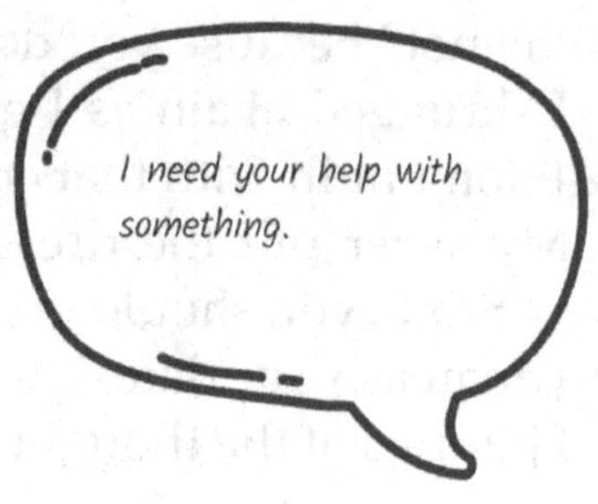

It took a minute before I received a response.

I took that as a positive sign and typed:

I clicked send and anxiously held my breath for a response. When it didn't readily come, I felt even more alone and faint-hearted. Another five minutes passed, and I couldn't take it anymore. Any longer, and my heart would've broken in half.

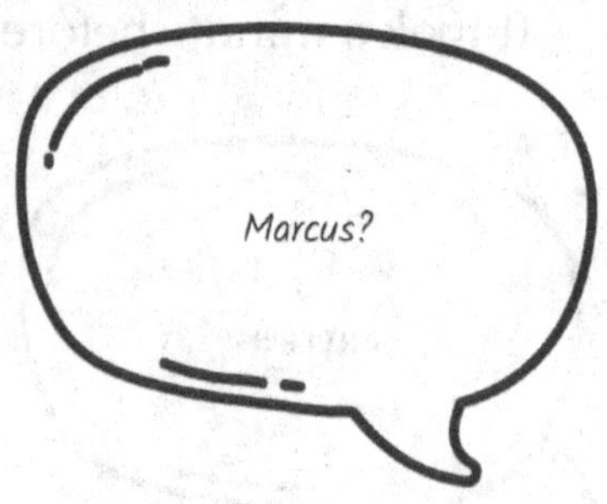

Dropping the phone on the bed, I decided to get ready to go to sleep instead of obsessing over an answer that I knew would be an emphatic no. Then the phone went off, and all of my *cool* points went out the window. I jumped on the bed to grab it, bounced right off the mattress, and landed on my back on the floor. The air escaped my lungs, but it didn't stop me from checking the phone.

I refused to start screaming until I knew for sure that it meant he would be my date. While I got myself off the floor, my parents barged into the room with similar petrified gazes.

"Bree, baby, what happened?"

"Are you alright, Brina?" Both my parents asked at

the same time.

I felt fine. After the operation, I sometimes got random headaches, but my stitches had dissolved, and the doctor had removed the one staple I had. There wasn't any permanent damage leftover from the accident, except a scar and a small bald spot where they did the surgery. My hair was thick, so it covered it without issue.

"Guys, I'm fine. I just fell off the bed."

Relieved, they walked back out of the room. I grabbed the phone and wrote Marcus back.

I bit my lip and waited.

Sweet Jesus! Is he going to do it?

Was he going to be my date for the dance?

All of the anxiety I felt flew out of the window. I couldn't be happier. I realized a few things at once. First, Marcus and I would meet for the first time, and second, he couldn't be lying to me because our first meeting was at my high school. Marcus agreed to be my date for Prom. What if he was extremely handsome and I made the other girls jealous? I mentally slapped myself. It didn't matter. We'd never spoken about our looks, but I was sure he was handsome. I had already fallen for the man on the other end of the line. Even if I was the only one wearing the rose-colored glasses, there wasn't anyone who could make me think any differently.

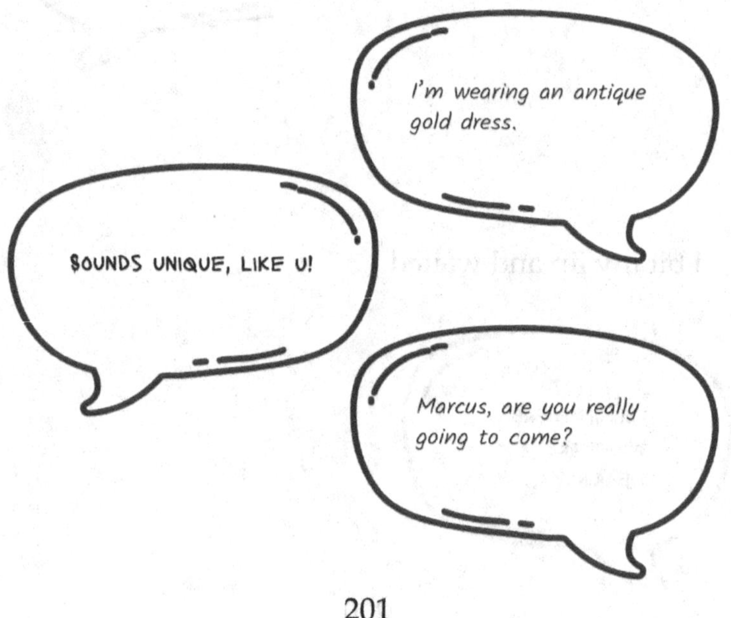

There was only a brief silence before the phone went
back off.

Yes.
I didn't know then, but that one word would change
me forever.

Dylan Marcus Taylor

THE WEEK WENT by faster than I would have ever expected. I filmed the new movie in Paris that week. Robin made sure my schedule was jam-packed during the week to fly back in time for Brina's school Prom. This time I wouldn't let her down. I cared about this girl and may have even fallen for her.

I remembered getting the message from Bree to come to the hospital. She was finally alright with me seeing her like that, but I couldn't bring myself to go. It wouldn't be a good time to tell her I was Dylan Taylor with her being in the hospital. I didn't want to put pressure on her injuries. It scared me to think that I might have made things worse if I did go.

But because I couldn't stay away, I did go back to the hospital as Dylan with my cousin June to see her again. We only got to stay there for an hour before we both had to go due to visiting schedules.

It was the best hour of my life.

I told June about the mystery girl being Brina and how I had met her before at the premiere of Breathless and then again at the fragrance unveiling. June was ecstatic to know that the woman he had initially approved of was the one I had been talking to from the very beginning. And more so because I was slowly falling head over foot. I got on the airplane that would take me back to the Hub because it felt too long since I'd left my hometown.

Robin sat beside me in first class. The woman may have been my agent, but she was also my manager and lawyer. That was the plus side of being her only client. I gave her enough work to keep her incredibly busy. She wasn't too keyed-up about the crazy news that would come out the day after showing up at Bree's Prom, but she knew how to twist it enough to give me significant press—even though I wasn't doing it for that reason.

Our potential relationship had nothing to do with anyone but her and me. I cared about Bree and wanted the world to know that Dylan Taylor knew how to pick them right. No more paparazzi connecting me to Vanessa Dallas in any way. If my fans were dying to see who I was dating, I wanted them to see me with Brina Palace. Both me and Robin were ready for the news that would come out of this and had a plan prepared to protect Brina and her family should it be necessary.

After texting Bree that I would go, I was so happy I immediately ran into my closet to see if I had anything that matched her dress choice. I had never been to a Prom but knew that couples dressed similarly to one another. I would do anything in my power to try and make it a dream come true for my Bree.

Inside the massive closet, I found a black tuxedo I had worn to the VMA Awards Ceremony a while back. The cut was flattering, so I walked over to my dress shirts and carefully sought the right one. I found a pearl-colored shirt and paired it with the tuxedo. The colors favored one another, but something was missing. I grabbed some antique gold cuff-links and a black bow tie.

I'd found the right choice.

I walked out of the closet and called for Nana. After I handed over the outfit to get pressed at the dry cleaners, I got on the phone with my florist and told her what I wanted. She said she could order a dull gold-colored rose for my jacket and one as a corsage for my date's wrist. I was excited about the ensemble I was picturing in my mind. I quickly got on the phone with my people to get everyone up to date.

That's how I spent the next few days. Working overseas for my new movie, I worked day and night, barely slept, but I knew that once I got on the plane, I could shut my eyes and catch up on my sleep. Things were going as planned until someone I never expected to show up on set came to see me. Vanessa, dressed in tight, form-fitting skinny jeans with knee-high boots, a black, drooped-knit top, and a Parisian scarf around her neck, came into view.

I was on a fifteen-minute break, so I had marched on over to her. "Vanessa, what are you doing here?"

She ran her long fingernails down my costume, made up of trousers and button-down with a tie hanging off my neck.

"I came to see you, silly," she practically purred.

I removed her hands and set them down, feeling better now that she was no longer touching me. "I don't recall asking you to come."

She pouted her full lips at me. "I'm here as part of your support group. My new movie doesn't start filming yet, and I should be supporting my guy, right?"

Her guy?

She must've been planning something because this was the first time I'd heard of it. I grabbed her arm as gently as I could compared to the heated blood in my veins and walked her off to the side with me. "What do you want, Vanessa? We aren't dating anymore and haven't been for over a year."

Vanessa took her loose arm and wrapped it around my neck. "We could be back on. Admit we're perfect for one another." She coyly stuck her body close to mine.

I pulled back from her clutches and told her with all honest sincerity. "I'm not looking to date you again, Vanessa."

She was unperturbed by the news. "I won't take no for an answer. Us being together would bring great publicity and more job offers."

One side of my mouth lifted in a devilish grin. "So you're just using me?"

She winked. "Now you're catching on sexy." She stole a kiss from my lips. I put my hands on her body to push her from me. She walked away. "Catch you later, Dylan."

I stood motionless. The girl was utterly insane if she thought I would play the same game she was playing. I had already dated the girl once, and once was more than enough. Besides, I was very much looking forward to starting a relationship with Brina. She was the girl I talked to every morning and the one I said good night to before I went to bed.

I wiped at my mouth with a handkerchief, making sure to remove any lipstick from my lips. The producer, Jacque, came around from the back and sat down with me.

"The girl is your *amour, oui*?" the producer asked.

I shook my head before he had even finished talking. "Nope, just a girl I used to date."

"*Elle obsédé*?" he asked in French.

If my French was spot on, which I knew it was, the producer had asked me if she was obsessed with me.

I smiled at Jacque, "God, I hope not!"

Jacque took out a pack of cigarettes and smoked one. I was glad I didn't smoke. The stuff was foul-smelling, and I was a very health-conscious person. Anything wrong for me, like cigarettes and Vanessa Dallas, I kept far away from me.

Jacque smoked his cigarette while watching Vanessa from afar. "Elle *beau*."

I had to agree with Jacque. Vanessa *was* beautiful but not my ideal woman. I liked girls with substance, smarts, and genuine dispositions. Bree was the type of girl I wanted.

The day had gone on, and we finished in time for me to leave to the states early, get to the Prom, and finally hold Brina in my arms. I was looking forward to it all day long.

The sound of engines starting up brought me back into the present. I sat back in the ivory-colored seats of the airline and relaxed. It was only Friday evening, so I had plenty of time to get back into the states before the Prom. Everything was going according to plan until the captain came over the intercom to tell us that we had mechanical problems and would not be leaving at our scheduled departure time. The news sent my head spinning. This dilemma was not what I wanted to happen, regardless of what was going on with the plane. The crew needed to fix things fast because I had a schedule and a promise to keep.

Damn!

Brina Palace

THE PARTY WAS in full swing as students arrived inside the hotel hall we were holding the Prom in. The room's decorations resembled a black and white movie, with black and white photographs enlarged to full-size and scattered throughout the interior of the banquet hall. The photos were of different seniors throughout the year in a variety of fun poses. Some students blew kisses to the camera while others put up the peace sign. Most were in groups that consisted of after-school clubs or large groups of friends.

This idea brought an authentic flair to the Prom's

decorative look. Black tablecloths adorned the round tables throughout the hall with white cloth napkins, and white bows tied to each chair. The disc jockey played an eclectic mixture of music with multi-colored lights shining on the dance floor to the beat of the bass. Juniors and seniors danced together in magnificent gowns and dashing tuxedos. Some of them shuffled around the floor while others gyrated to the music. One side of the hall had a professional photographer. He snapped pictures of couples and groups of best friends. Beside the professional photographer's station stood a photo booth for the students to take fun photos together on a film that came out saying "Prom Memories 2022" on the bottom.

The other side of the enormous hall had banquet tables standing side by side with refreshments on one end and lots of platters of food and hors d'oeuvre's on the other. Kids stood all over the place enjoying themselves, except for me. I stood all alone without a date. My sister danced with her boyfriend, so I snapped another photo of the couple. I snapped more pictures of the rest of the students parading on the dance floor with the camera I had borrowed from the school yearbook staff.

I shouldn't have felt so upset, but I was devastated. Marcus should've been here as promised, but he didn't show up. I shouldn't have been surprised. He was probably someone other than who he made himself out to be, and I was a fool for believing in him. Marcus was to meet me at eight o'clock in the middle of the dance floor, and like an idiot, I waited. I had left him a ticket at the front so he could claim his invite.

Like a fool, I thought things would work and that he would be there for me. But Marcus didn't show up at all. I stood in the middle of the dance floor for half an hour before I decided to get moving.

Instead of feeling more like a fool, I did my best work for the yearbook committee and snapped many excellent photographs. An hour later, from our scheduled time, I walked to the lobby to see if Marcus claimed the ticket or if I had messages. Nothing. The card was still there. Unclaimed. There were also no messages left for me. I had left the cell phone—not finding a suitable spot on my dress to hide it. Either way, I had told Marcus I wouldn't have it on me. I asked him what he was wearing or how I would recognize him should he come. He let me know I couldn't miss him. Marcus would be straightforward to spot.

Easy or not, I didn't see him anywhere in the hall. I glanced over at the clock on the wall, seeing that it was already nine-thirty at night. Resolved to forget about Marcus, I moved from my spot against the wall to take more photographs. They had announced the King and Queen for Prom, and I went trigger happy, snapping photos of Stefan and my sister Estella, who had won the crown. Homecoming Queen and Prom Queen, my sister Estella was quite the collector of crowns. After snapping the last photos I needed for the yearbook committee, I went over to the teacher in charge and handed the camera to him.

"All done, Miss Bree?"

I replied with a smile. "Yes, sir. I've got hundreds of photos to choose from. The night is almost over, so I'm probably going to go home now."

He frowned, "Not finishing the night?"

I shook my head. He nodded and let me go. I heard Estella's favorite song come out of the loudspeakers, so I walked toward the dance floor where I knew my sister would be. Looking once more at the clock on the wall, it read ten after ten that night. Estella shook her hips with her king on the middle of the dance floor.

The students jostled me to and fro as I squeezed between the couples. Mable got caught on another student's fake gemstones, which decorated the lower part of her cocktail dress. I stopped moving, afraid Mable would rip. So far, Mable had been nothing but bad luck. I was continually tripping over it, or it was getting stuck to things I passed by. Plus, I wasn't meeting my true love any time soon.

There was only bad luck for me.

"Ugh, get your ugly dress off of my jewels."

Great, it was just my luck.

I bent over and removed the loose thread from the caught stone. "See, all better."

I went to walk away when the girl decided I hadn't had enough.

"Why are you here, junior? You look pathetic."

I felt as pathetic as she claimed. Instead of retreating, I swallowed the massive knot in my throat and put down my head to hide my red face. I took deep breaths to calm myself. I made a promise not to let these vultures get me down. Most of the students stopped focusing on me after the accident, but some couldn't take the hint. They had nothing else in their lives going for them. That's what small town life did to some people.

"Say something, dork! Or are you hiding behind

Guy and your sister Estella now?"

I shook my head and put a hand up to stop Estella from rushing over. "My sister and Guy have nothing to do with this."

"By the way, thought you should know that Guy is using you. Your family could've sued his fat ass, but he is kissing yours to stay on the football team."

I paled in the face of her ignorance. "You can think whatever you want."

The girl snapped. She decided to use more underhanded tactics when she couldn't get a significant enough reaction from me. This time she nudged me with her hand, sending me back a step or two. "You don't belong here. Stop trying to be something you're not."

"Don't worry your pretty little head about it. I'll leave. I wouldn't want your special night ruined," I taunted sarcastically with a roll of my eyes.

Gasps came from the entire hall of kids. Students stopped moving and dancing altogether. Others stopped eating as food lay untouched on their forks. They were silent as they stared in my general direction or rather at the something standing behind me.

Did I say something rude? Am I getting in trouble?

Anxiety trickled down my spine as student after student shuffled to each side as if parting like the Red Sea. Students snapped photos with their camera phones, others gleefully murmured, and the rest stared in wide-eyed shock.

"I would at least hope to get one dance, Brina Palace," I heard a male voice say from behind me.

I recognized that voice. Girls shrieked. Goosebumps

ran down my spine. But...

I slowly turned around to see the last person I'd ever expect at a regular high-school promenade. Dylan Taylor stood in front of me in an immaculate tuxedo with a pearl-colored dress shirt and dull gold—almost bronze-tinted cufflinks. He had a pale gold rose pinned to his lapel and a small box in his hand with a gold ribbon tied around it. His smile was sweet, and his hair was slicked back with a slight curl around his ear. Dylan was so handsome it hurt to watch.

"W-what are you doing here?"

Dylan grinned wider. "I believe I was invited."

I went speechless.

Did Estella invite him to the Prom? I figured Estella would sway Dylan. The pretty girls always got their way. Guess it was too much to hope that Estella would have given me a heads up, at least. Speaking of Estella, she appeared beside a group of girls as surprised as the rest.

"Did Estella invite you?" Before I even finished, Estella shook her head.

He smiled again and took a step closer to me, sending my heart soaring to new heights I didn't even know existed.

"You invited me."

Did I? When did I do that? My head injury was recent, but I didn't recall making that invitation, and I sure as heck wouldn't have forgotten it. I let go of a breath I didn't know I was holding while murmurs went on around the hall.

He snickered and put his hand out to shake mine. "Hello, Brina Palace. I'm Dylan Marcus Taylor."

I numbly shook his hand, still at a loss on what was going on. Dylan Marcus Taylor said that I had invited him to the Prom when I didn't remember… Dylan. Marcus. Taylor. Dylan… Marcus…

Oh my god!

Before I said anything, he added, "I believe you have my phone."

Finally registering his full name, my jaw dropped.

"M-Marcus?"

One side of his mouth lifted in a mischievous grin. "Hi, Bree."

My knees went weak, but Marcus, or instead Dylan, was there to grab hold of me around the waist. His arm felt strong as it wrapped around me to hold me in place securely. Everything made sense now. June from the phone was Juniel, his cousin. VD was Vanessa Dallas. All of the trips overseas and the regular work schedule. I should've known all of these *in my face* things by putting the most straightforward clues together. I stared at the man I had been talking to for weeks. How could I have not known? All of those things I said to him! All of the things he said to me. The "surprise" visit to the hospital. I blinked from all I tried to process at one time.

"I got this for you."

He let go of my waist the moment I was steady. He opened the box to reveal a beautiful gold rose wrapped in stretchy lace. *A corsage?* He got me a corsage like an actual date to the Prom would. I didn't even register the people around me anymore. I only saw Dylan and me. He put the rose on my wrist and signaled the DJ to keep playing. Paramore's *All I Wanted* blared from the speakers, so Dylan grabbed my hand to guide me to the center of the dance floor. He took my sweaty palms and put them around his neck. With my hands locked behind his neck, I unconsciously ran my fingers through his dark hair. He shivered, wrapping his arms around my waist. Dylan pulled me closer to him. We both swayed from side to side as other couples followed suit, some taking pictures while others chose to dance beside us.

"You look beautiful in that dress."

This moment had to be a dream. I was dancing at Prom with the man I had fallen head over heels for through text. How did I not make the connection between Dylan and Marcus? I knew Dylan had a middle name that started with an M, but I didn't make the connection. Why would I ever think that a sliver of a cell phone would ever belong to famous superstar Dylan Taylor? He pulled me closer to him as another song played in the background. Dylan smelled so good; I refused to let go of him. A student tapped his shoulder, and he turned to regard her. For a second, I lost myself in his embrace. When the girl touched his shoulder, the dream broke, and reality set in. He was a superstar that always put his fan's needs before his own.

"No autographs right now, okay?" He winked at her, and she resembled melted chocolate on the dance floor. She nodded and walked away in awe. Did he send her away?

He ran his hand up and down my back. "Right now, I belong to you," he said to me.

"This just can't be happening to me." I must've fallen on my face after tripping over Mable. I had to be dreaming this up.

He pulled me away from him, and I immediately felt bereft. "Bree, I'm here for you and you only. You understand?"

The beautiful actor's dark eyes seemed so severe that I could do nothing but nod and smile. "You're late, Dylan."

He laughed. "Aw, sweetheart, I'm so sorry. They delayed my flight a few hours."

My entire body vanished at the use of the endearment.

"I never meant to be late."

I believed him. It was a little late, but I finally realized that good things do happen in this dress. Mable was my good luck charm. Wait until I told Reba about my night. Mable made true to her promise of helping her owner find true love.

Dylan Marcus Taylor

I HURRIED AROUND my room, collecting my wallet and phone. It was Sunday morning and my last day of freedom before I had to rush back to Europe for filming. Last night had gone great with Bree. We danced to a few songs and took pictures in the photo booth and with the professional photographer. I made sure to capture any of the memories I could with her.

She was so beautiful in that classical piece she wore. The dress fit her like a glove as it molded to every curve of her exquisite body. Her natural beauty enthralled me. She made me happy on so many levels that I couldn't contain the ever-present smile on my face. I drove her home at around midnight and was embarrassed because I couldn't stop acting like a bumbling fool around her. I smiled as I remembered.

The walk from my car to her front door felt long as I tried to keep my swagger in check and instead ended up tripping over one of the laid-out bricks that made up her pathway. I stumbled but remained upright. Bree stood beside me with mirth in her eyes and a slight smirk on her rosy lips. I pinched her nose and grinned. We finally made it to her front door, and I fell all over myself trying to be smooth and swoop in for a kiss.

Again, I failed miserably.

Like I did in my movies, we slowly came together. Unfortunately, just as I was about to press my lips to hers, Bree's father turned the front light off and on in rapid succession. We both jumped apart like opposite sides of a magnet. I shook my head, remembering the fear and anxiety I felt at that moment. Bree had laughed at me again while her father poked his head out the door. He gave me a calculated look—one that I was sure was meant to spark fear deep in my belly and then gave his daughter a look that uttered, "come inside."

I came back to the present and focused on the task at hand. I ran down the stairs, waved goodbye to Nana, but stopped short of the front stoop in front of my brownstone. The sidewalk in front of my building had crowded with all sorts of media and paparazzi. When they saw me, they took several pictures of me in front of the home. I took my sunglasses off the side table by the door and shielded my eyes from the sun and the blinding flashes of their cameras. Brandon was already in front of my door, moving people to the side as I walked toward my car.

Damn.

I knew they would go nuts because of my appearance at the NorthEnd High prom, but I wasn't expecting the massive amount of bodies shoving back and forth to get a photo of me. The paparazzi pushed microphones, tape recorders, and video cameras in front of my face.

"Dylan, is it true that you were seen last night at a NorthEnd High's school Prom?" asked one reporter.

Another yelled over the first, "Our sources claim that you were there for a girl—a Brina Palace, high-school junior."

Knowing what I was going to say, I stopped short of reaching the car parked out front. My bodyguard pushed a reporter that got too close to the side. "I would appreciate it if you left Brina and her family alone. Whatever questions you may have will be answered by Robin Fellows, my agent. She has all the details. At this present time, Brina and her family are off-limits until she or they say otherwise."

The questions kept coming, but I ignored them and got inside my car. The first thing I did before turning on the car was to call Bree. I linked my phone to Bluetooth and dialed the phone number. The line rang a few times with no answer. I clicked "end" on the call and started the car. My phone then went off on my lap.

Damn, Dylan. I thought to myself. *How could I not remember that?*

I clicked send and waited a few minutes to assure myself that she had received it. I pressed dial again and waited for her to pick up before heading out on the road. The paparazzi tried to knock on my window, but Brandon stood in front of my door and shooed them away. Brandon was always there to protect me. The man was almost four-hundred pounds of muscle at nearly six-foot-five. No one could get that man down. As I moved, my bodyguard got into his SUV to follow behind me like he always did. Close at hand, but far enough for privacy.

"Hello?" I heard her voice and had to contain myself so I didn't turn to a pile of goo.

Putting the car in gear, I placed both hands on the wheel and maneuvered around the hoard of people. "Hey, gorgeous. Good morning."

I could almost see her smiling on the other end of the line. "Good morning, Dylan."

I took a turn down the street to get on the Highway 93 ramp. "Have the media bothered you guys today?"

Her breathy laugh sent shivers down my spine. "It's all good. My dad is a lawyer. He got legal on them real quick."

I audibly sighed. "I'm sorry, sweetheart. I've already spoken to my agent, and she will make sure to get things handled. I was going to talk to you last night about what to expect today, but being with you had me turning into a wicked fool."

She giggled again. "Quit exaggerating, and don't worry. I haven't talked to the press, so you can be sure I don't say the wrong thing like we're dating or something."

For some reason, I was upset she'd think that. "Bree, why would you think our dating would be the wrong thing to say?"

I heard her mumble something to someone in the background and then come back to the phone. "Sorry about that. Estella asked me if I've looked out the window today. She had to honk the horn to get back into the driveway. Dad got them off our property, but the sidewalk is fair game."

I signaled a driver that I was getting in the fast lane.

"Bree, I'm on my way to see you now, but...." I trailed off when she spoke to me.

"You're on your way here now?" she squeaked.

The car in front of me barely limped along. I put on the brakes as the car slowed down. "Yeah, that's why I called you so early. Besides, I told you I was coming by last night," I reminded her.

"Yeah, but I didn't know it was going to be now. I'm not even dressed, Dylan Marcus Taylor!" she scolded.

I laughed as I teased her. "Nice. Does that mean I get to see the infamous teddy?"

She made a sharp, high-pitched sound over the phone. "Dylan! Oh, you're mighty fresh this morning," she mumbled self-consciously.

I enjoyed seeing her blush and could only imagine how she looked like right now. "Curious, sweetheart. Mighty curious."

"Whatever, Dylan. I'm going to let you go now because I need to get changed."

I snorted.

"Alright, I'll see you in a few minutes." We hung up the line at the same time.

Maneuvering around another car, I increased my speed. I hoped Bree felt the same way about me that I did about her because I didn't know what to do if she didn't want to have any part of the life of a celebrity. I was so concerned about my wants that I didn't stop to think about all of the consequences that came along with being my girlfriend. I was ready to protect her and her family, but was I willing to feed her to the wolves? I was at the top of my career. At a pinnacle point, every star wanted to achieve success, and every fan and brand wanted a piece of them.

Refusing to think any more sad thoughts, I drove to

Brina's house.

I ARRIVED AT Brina's house precisely forty minutes later and was now sitting on her parlor room
couch with a rod-stiff Bree sitting right beside me. She
was freshly showered and smelled like the strawberry
shampoo she used in her long dark hair. When I arrived on the little road that went to her house, I could
see the plethora of paparazzi parked out front. When
I turned the corner, they snapped pictures of my car
arriving at her residence. I parked in the driveway,
knowing Mr. Palace had already made sure they did
not step foot on his property. I got out of my car with
the shades in place.

The cameras flashed, and the media personnel hollered for me to give them a statement. I ignored them
as I made my way to her door. Turning on the tiny
cobblestone path, I saw Brandon approach and park
down the street from my peripheral. I sighed, visibly
more relaxed now that I knew Brandon would make
sure no one entered the property illegally. Ringing
the doorbell, I waited only mere seconds before Estella poked her head out. She was immaculately dressed
and made-up. The female ushered me inside and led
me to the parlor room, where I sat and listened to a
very educated and over-protective father reading me
my rights.

"Daaaad!" Bree hollered for the third time.

"Brina, baby, if this young man wants to date my

daughter, then he needs to prove to me that his intentions are pure."

I felt Bree stiffen even more beside me. Estella hovered in the background, and her mother sat in a lounge chair, listening in and every so often adding her two cents. I enjoyed this. There wasn't a time where I remembered sitting in a girlfriend's parlor room, hearing from the parents about how I should or shouldn't treat their daughter. I cared about Bree. Everything they told me, I already knew. My intentions were serious with the young woman—not all fun and games.

"Bree, it's alright. I respect your parents and like them, only want the best for you." I turned to grab her hand.

Locking our fingers together, I saw the blush adorn her cheeks, and her darker than jade eyes glossed over. Placing our interlocked hands on my knee, I turned to face her parents. "I care about, Bree. I'm not here on a publicity stunt or a voyeur of young women. I'm serious about her."

I saw Mr. Palace nod and lean forward. "Good, because my baby girl deserves the best, and she seems to think you are it, Mr. Taylor."

Her mom added, "You're a mega superstar, Dylan. We just wanted her to know what she was getting herself into."

I immediately felt a sharp pang in my chest because I knew her parents were only protecting her, but I feared Bree would realize being with me would be much too hard. I straightened and faced her parents. "I understand your concerns, and I agree."

I turned to Bree.

"Sweetheart, you know how I feel about you. It won't be easy being my girlfriend, and the last thing I want to do is hurt you. I need you to be sure."

If it was possible, Bree sat even straighter with her cute little chin jutting out in a sign of defiance. In that instant, I knew there was no mistaking my feelings for this little vixen who stole my heart over text.

She exhaled long and hard before she said, "I'll admit. At first, I thought that this was all a dream or a figment of my imagination, but the realization of what is happening between us is real. I know exactly what I am getting into."

Bree turned to face me. "And I'm not about to run away and hide because a few paparazzi want to camp out on my lawn."

"Damn right," Estella whooped from her spot.

We laughed.

My heart melted as her eyes stared back into mine once the humor was gone. At that moment, all I wanted to do was take her in my arms and kiss her silly. I refrained from embarrassing myself in front of her family.

"Please also understand, Dylan, that our baby girl is only seventeen."

Bree's face went red before they even finished what they were saying to me.

"You are wise with the world. Brina isn't."

Damn. Is this the sex talk?

Pressing my lips tighter together to prevent a laugh from coming out, I watched her parents unconsciously embarrass their youngest daughter. Bree seemed about ready to pass out.

Using my free hand, I made the gesture to stop her parents from continuing. "Mr. and Mrs. Palace, I'm not dating Bree with specific…." I waved my hand around as I tried to figure out the right word to say. I settled on "expectations" and took another deep breath. "I respect your daughter. I hope you understand that."

Bree let out a groan, so I gently squeezed her hand. Her parents faced her, waiting for her to respond to the conversation. Her bright green eyes stared at her parents as she said, "I'm sure of what I want. I'll still be the same old Brina."

"Well, alright then. We respect your decision." Her father stood from the chair and walked over to me with his hand extended. "A pleasure meeting you, Mr. Taylor."

We shook hands. Bree had stood when I did to hug her father. I felt cold and empty when she moved to the side to allow her mother to get closer to me. The woman opened her arms and drew me into a hug. I felt encompassed by the family, absorbing how a colossal family was supposed to function for the first time in a long time. Nana, Charlie, and June were the only family I had left. They were my small circle. Joining Bree's family just made that circle double in size and if I screwed it up with Bree, losing them too would be a huge blow emotionally. Estella came over to me next and wrapped her arms around me as well.

She let go as she whispered in my ear. "Hurt her, and you die, Dylan."

I tried not to laugh out loud as I dropped my arms when she let go. Yes, losing Bree and her family would break me in more ways than one.

Bree's family finally left the room, one by one. The first thing I did was pull her into my arms where she fit perfectly into the mold of my body. She clung to me as tightly as she could, finally relaxing her petite frame as I held her.

I slowly pulled her away from me to stare at her face. She blinked repeatedly. I could see where she rushed to put on mascara and knowing she felt the need to even get prettier for me when I was already so enthralled with her made my heart pound even more. My face moved toward hers. Her eyes widened when I was finally able to taste her lips. Pressing mine tighter to hers, the world around me could have gone up in smoke, and I wouldn't have noticed. She tasted of cherry Chapstick. Forcing myself to pull away, I stared at her radiant face. She had a light dusting of freckles over her cheekbones and nose. Brina's emerald eyes shone brighter, and it made me want to pull her in for another kiss, only to see them glow like that again.

"I've wanted to do that for a long time."

She didn't say anything. Her lips were still moist from our kiss. Afraid I may have overstepped a boundary somewhere; I opened my mouth to apologize. Bree didn't allow me the chance when she pulled me down to her height again and kissed me senselessly. We pulled apart again to take a breath, but the taste of her made me lick my lips in response.

She grinned like a naughty little kitten. "I've wanted to do *that* for a long time."

I laughed. Brina grabbed my hand and led me out of the parlor room. Passing a demented miniature poodle along the way, Bree led me up the stairs toward a room to our left. Recognizing it as a bedroom, I got my first glimpse of a real, everyday teenage girl's room.

Bree's room was clean, with her bed already made. The only thing that seemed out of place was a clicker on top of the bed and a pile of books on her desk. She didn't have posters of me in her bedroom, which was a relief. Pictures in frames adorned her walls of her achievements or accomplishments and some of her and her family. I walked inside and sat on her bed, testing the mattress's firmness. Leaning back on the bed, I perused her room. She sat crossed leg beside me and grinned.

"I cannot believe you are sitting on the bed in my room."

I was the picture of relaxation as I made myself comfortable on her floral bedspread, locking my ankles one over the other. I gave her one of my more sly smiles, one that I used in my more recent movies. Many women would swoon or bask in this particular smile, but not my Bree.

"Nice try, buddy. Get your feet off the bed." She made a slap for my feet as she giggled at the incredulous look on my face.

I sat up straighter and stared at the woman sitting next to me. "Thank you, Bree."

She tilted her head slightly to the side. "For what?"

Caressing her cheek, I pushed a stray strand behind her ear and leaned in to kiss her forehead. I could see the blush adorning her face and felt something tighten in my chest. "For not pushing me away when you found out who I was."

She wrinkled her nose while biting her full bottom

lip. "To be honest, I didn't think I was awake. I thought it all to be a dream until I saw the media on my lawn this morning. Then it kind of just felt surreal." She took my hand in her own, squeezing my fingers tightly. "I don't know why you chose me, Dylan, but I can't let what I feel slip through my fingers. No harm in trying, right?"

I leaned in for another kiss. In the rich and famous world, especially in the circle where we actors find ourselves, we straddle a blurred line between reality and fiction. I always prided myself in knowing the difference between the two, which allowed me this modicum of freedom. Falling in love on set never translated to my relationships outside of work. I never used the word love before on any woman other than my Nana, but I was more than sure I'd end up using it on her.

Brina Palace

I WALKED THE halls of the school, finally seeking a few minutes of solace for myself. Students snickered behind my back. Others were happy with my relationship, while the rest only wanted to get close to the girl with a famous boyfriend. Either way, I was tired of all the attention I had received the past few days. Monday was the worst of it. On Sunday night, the media played the recorded interview Dylan Taylor had agreed to do to appease them.

Dylan had asked me if I would join him outside to speak to the paparazzi. "Once they get what they want," he began, "they will drop it and leave your family alone."

Making sure he held my hand the entire time to feel safe, I walked outside and stood next to Dylan as he spoke to the press. I agreed to do the interview with him. They asked questions about how we met, to which he replied: "At my Breathless premiere."

Nothing more, nothing less.

They asked him everything. "Are you both in a serious relationship?"

Dylan had squeezed my hand tightly. "Yes."

"Are you in love with her?"

He smiled at the cameras, using one of his assorted seductive grins. "If you let us explore our relationship, I'll let you know."

"Why did you choose her over all of the beautiful women in your life, including Vanessa Dallas?"

He didn't even stutter. "Because not only is Ms. Palace beautiful as well but exceptionally down to earth and beyond kind," he said as he stared into my eyes.

They bombarded us with question after question, and he fed them straight answers without adding more information that didn't concern them but made it seem like they got the scoop of a lifetime. The way he handled the press enthralled me. He had asked them to leave my family and me alone as a favor to him. The press got their questions answered and left my property happy. Dylan Taylor had such an effect on the public that they would keel over to fulfill his requests.

I returned his phone before he left on Sunday, even though he initially refused to take it. I already had a phone, and it was about time he took his back. I made a promise to call him whenever the urge struck and never to forget that it was this little bit of technology that helped our relationship grow. I exchanged numbers with Dylan to continue our romance over the phone. After all, it was over the phone that we had grown to care for one another.

Needing to go over the projects for the New England Restoration, I entered the door to the central office, where some of the members waited. After a couple of minutes of them trying to pry into my relationship or get Dylan to join the vital cause, we got down to business and divided the new load of projects between the members.

Finally finished, I headed down the walkway of the school to go home. Without a bicycle to ride, walking was my next viable option. Estella had her own business to attend to after school. Not that she ever gave me a ride before, but our relationship was better since the accident. After cheerleading practice, Estella did retail as her part-time job. If I wanted to earn some money to pay for things and dates, I would have to find a job myself.

With Monday behind me, and Tuesday ending on a better note, I walked past a group of females hanging around on the school grounds after practice. Out of curiosity, I looked around to see if Estella was still around. Not finding any sign of her, my attention turned to a few of the girls who snickered as I passed. One of the girls moved toward me.

It was the same girl from the prom. "It seems your little romance ended rather quickly. I said it would last one day, but some of the girls said two or more. I guess they were right."

"What are you talking about, Anna?" I sighed. I knew I should have just walked away like I always did when they were mean to me, but if I didn't start putting my foot down, they were never going to stop harassing me.

Anna grinned straight white teeth as she handed me a tabloid magazine. "My uncle works for this magazine and gave me an early copy of it."

I stared at the front cover. My heart took a nose dive into the deepest depths of my stomach and got lost in the emptiness somewhere. I couldn't seem to get it beating again as I felt darkness envelop me. It was a recent shot originating from his overseas movie location. Dylan Taylor kissed Vanessa Dallas. The kiss was on his mouth, on his lips. It was an actual kiss—a kiss that looked similar to the kisses he gave me. She clung to him. They both had their eyes closed, and his hands had settled on her hips.

From what I knew of his new movie shoot, Vanessa Dallas was not an actress on the set. This predicament meant she had flown over to visit him. Maybe he didn't want me to know he was caught up in an on-screen off-screen romance with her. Another picture lower on the page showed a very tired and embarrassed me walking out of class. I almost balled the paper in my hand. One of my many enemies was happy to provide that picture to the press.

The headlines on the trashy tabloid read, *Brina who? Vanessa rekindles her romance with Dylan.*

I handed the magazine back to Anna and refused to let her see that her attack on me worked. I smiled to hide the pain I felt inside and walked away.

Anna called out, "So you're okay with Vanessa and Dylan getting it on?"

I waved my hand as I walked farther away from the menacing crowd, suddenly aware that I was not as beautiful as Vanessa Dallas and certainly not as glamorous.

Halfway home, I couldn't stop the tears from falling down my face. Was Dylan cheating on me with Vanessa? Did he care about me like he claimed, or was he that much of a great actor? Scared of the correct answer, I pulled out my phone to look at the time. It was probably around ten-thirty at night where he was, so I sent him a text with shaking fingers.

I put my phone back in my pocket, continuing my trek back home. My Converse clad-feet dragged on the floor, hoping that no new surprises arose. A car horn pulled me away from my moping, so I turned my head to see Estella riding alongside me in her little red bug.

"Sup, sis. Need a ride?" I would rather walk, but I was also slightly shocked that my sister even offered.

Didn't she have to go to work today? Did her cheerleading friends tell her about the tabloid?

I shook my head and kept walking. My sister pulled up farther down the street and stopped the car. She got out of the vehicle, and with worried eyes, concern etching her features, she asked me what was wrong.

I didn't realize I was still crying and most certainly didn't even realize when I ran to my sister and buried myself in her chest to cry. Estella tried to calm me, but I couldn't seem to get the tears to stop flowing. She pulled me away and stared right into my eyes.

"Talk to me, Brina. Does your head hurt?"

I shook my head. "Anna…" I started to cry again.

Estella went off on a roar. "What the heck did that spoiled little brat do to you?"

The thing was that she didn't do anything to me. All she did was show me a magazine about to come out tomorrow for the world to see my boyfriend and his ex-girlfriend making out.

I calmed the flow of tears enough to speak. "Anna showed me a tabloid that is going to come out tomorrow."

Estella's thin eyebrow rose.

"The picture in the front had Dylan and Vanessa in a kissing embrace."

"What?"

I nodded. "It's recent, Estella. He is overseas filming a movie, and I know Vanessa is not a part of the project, yet there she was." I told her as my arms fell to the sides.

"I'll kill him!" Estella loyally screamed.

Just as I was about to agree, the phone went off in my pocket. I pulled it out, trying to control the trembling in my hands.

Taking a deep, calming breath of fresh air, I typed.

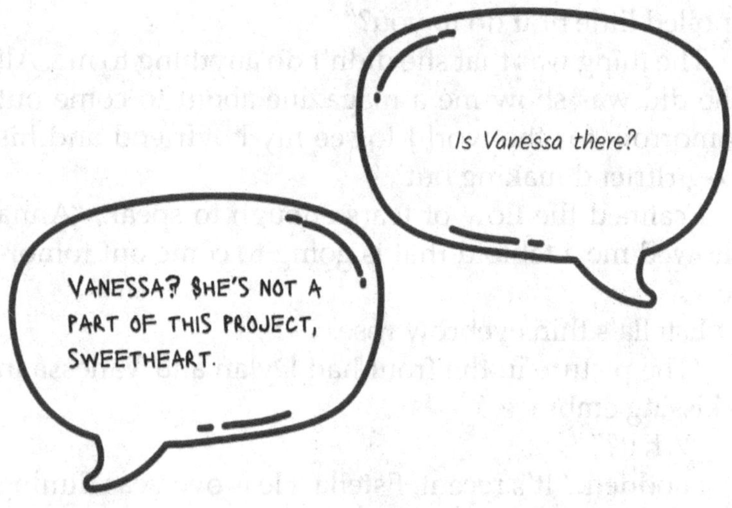

Estella waved me toward the car, using her hand to gesture to the front passenger side as a car model. A rare smile at my sister's teasing flitted across my lips. Shaking my head, I got into the car with Estella and texted Dylan on our way home.

I took a fortifying breath.

After I hit send, a minute went by, and my phone rang as I exited Estella's car. I waved my sister inside so that I could take the call outside in privacy. I answered the call with a knot of nerves in my throat. What if he was calling me all pissed off at getting caught? What if the picture wasn't what it seemed, and he was mad that I didn't trust him? Fear took root in my belly as I pressed the answer button on my phone. I didn't even get a standard greeting before I heard Dylan's sexy voice on the other end of the line.

"What picture, Bree?"

I took another deep breath. "I thought you couldn't call."

People chatted in a background that sounded farther and farther away. "When my girl texts me that she saw me kiss another woman, I tell the directors to give me a five-minute break."

"So, it will only take you five minutes to resolve this little problem?" His calm tone of voice pissed me off. Was five minutes all it took for him to make this all go away? Doesn't he understand how painful it is for me to see the man I care about kissing other women who weren't his co-stars?

He laughed. Was the jerk seriously laughing at me? "Baby, it will once I tell you that it was most likely a retouched photo or an old picture."

Is he insulting my intelligence? Again? "Dylan, the picture was taken in France on your current shoot."

There was a brief silence, then more laughter. "Oh, sweetheart! I'm sorry...."

I exploded. "See! I knew it. Why apologize for something you did. I trusted you, Dylan."

"Sweetheart!"

I got quiet. Dylan's tone of voice changed instantly, and it made me shut my mouth. My Chucks picked at a plot of dirt on the grass.

"Brina Palace, are you jealous?"

I kicked the plot. "Of course not!"

Dylan took a deep breath, followed by him clearing his throat. "Bree, I'm not cheating on you. This stuff is what you will come to see often as my girlfriend. The press love to exaggerate what they think they see. I haven't seen any pictures of what you are talking about, but if I can recall correctly, it was when Vanessa came by the photoshoot and stole a kiss from me—after she explained that she was going to use me to gain some press before her new movie comes out."

I stared at my phone as if it grew legs and started walking. I felt ridiculous. Placing the phone back to my ear, I asked Dylan, "I'm supposed to believe that?"

"Honestly? Yes." he replied, clearly at wit's end.

I bit my lip. "Okay."

There was silence on the other end of the line, and I thought that I might have lost him there for a second. "Dylan?"

"You believe me?"

I smiled, hoping that I could convey how I felt over the phone. "Yes, I do. I have no reason not to, but I'm only human, Dylan Marcus. Next time tell me when something happens so that the press or ignorant teenagers do not ambush me."

He snickered. "I promise, babe." Someone called for him in the background. "Babe, I gotta go. Miss you."

"Miss you too, Marcus."

He laughed and hung up the phone.

Feeling much better, I skipped into the house. Tomorrow, when that magazine came out, and the world saw what I already knew, I needed all the strength I could muster to ignore the press that would surely be knocking on my door, and the crazy-ass females with vendettas they can't seem to shake off.

Dylan Marcus Taylor

THE AIR WAS colder than usual, and the night was clear enough to see all of the stars sparkling brightly above me. The tiny brilliant dots grew farther from my reach the farther I fell from the building I threw myself off. I felt the breath in my lungs escape the faster I descended toward the ground. The feeling of weightlessness covered me in a blanket of chills. I reached the spot where I could stop flailing my arms and crossed them over my chest. The landing pad finally hit my back. I had just been flipped over the building by one of my costars as the movie's last scenes got filmed.

Different set handlers helped me down as the assistant director maneuvered the large group of people diligently doing various tasks. The producer called it a wrap, sending all of us home for three days because the new filming starts in New York. These next three days were a much-needed break. I'd worked for two weeks straight without one. I missed my home, my bed, and my girlfriend.

After two weeks of dating Bree the press already tried linking me to the other woman. Vanessa worked her dark magic. She tried to get the world to think we were an item and that it hurt her seeing Bree and me together. I knew she was only doing it to gain press on her new movie, but this was my personal life she messed with. The picture Bree had texted me about a couple of weeks back had finally come out and indeed seemed like I kissed the girl back. I had my hands on her hips, but it wasn't because I was interested in touching her body—I just wanted to push her away, and my hands happened to be in that particular area.

I couldn't believe that Bree barely fussed over the disturbing picture. She was initially hurt, but I was glad she ultimately believed me. It surprised me because any other girl I dated would have started a fight over the phone, made me feel bad, and then I would feel forced to make it up to her. That route would ultimately result in a break-up.

These next three days would be spent making it up to Brina. Robin called me to advise that the jet was prepped for a late-night departure. The sooner I got back, the sooner I could enjoy my time with her.

AN UNPLEASANT CURRENT dropped me to the ground in agonizing pain. I could barely catch my breath before another blowing ache rendered me speechless. Knowing that I was utterly alone with a psychotic person, I tried to crawl away or scream for help. Nothing came out of my mouth. The deranged woman kicked me in the stomach again. This time, I hit the school's brick wall, holding my head from getting hurt but leaving everything else vulnerable to attack. The force dropped me to the ground. I couldn't see past my tears. After what seemed like a lifetime, I was finally able to scream for help—gratified to hear a male voice yelling at the female attacking me.

The young woman ran off as two burly teenage boys ran up to me. I could barely hear them over the ringing in my ears but thought I caught one tell the other to run after my assailant. I turned my head to see who held me in his arms and breathed a sigh of relief when I saw it was Guy. I watched one guy run off at breakneck speed as Guy scooped me up as if I weighed as much as a rag doll.

"Brina, are you hurt?"

I shook my head, afraid they would send me back to the hospital if I said yes.

He checked ahead of him and yelled out, "Hold her down, David."

David had the girl who attacked me pinned to

the ground. He pulled out his cellphone at the same time. After sitting me down on the school bench, Guy ran inside the building. I searched for my phone, but couldn't find it. I didn't even have my backpack. Just then, a tiny older woman ran out of the building, followed closely by Guy. I recognized her as the school nurse. A few minutes later, the cops arrived on the scene. After being checked by the nurse and the police, I spent another two hours on school grounds before I was allowed to go home with a few body aches and a bruise on my cheek by my chin—luckily nothing more.

The young woman was an enraged fan of the couple DyVa fandom—DyVa standing for Dylan and Vanessa. She was not happy to hear that I tried to get in between the relationship of her two favorite actors.

I knew the press would hound me, and I had to make do with women prancing around in skimpy outfits around my boyfriend—in addition to all that on-screen kissing or nudity. However, I was not ready for certifiably insane fans. After dealing with the police, Guy gave me a ride home. I was grateful I didn't have to walk back to my house in pain. The girl who attacked me was young, maybe about a year or two younger than me. She didn't have much weight on me, but she was quick, and it blindsided me.

I remember walking out the school's side door with my book bag over my shoulder, and seeing a young girl with Dylan and Vanessa's faces kissing on her shirt come up to me. She called me all sorts of names and then proceeded to throw water at my face, momentarily blinding me. In the instant it took me to wipe the water from my face, the DyVa groupie had pulled me down to the ground by my hair and kneed me on the side of my face. The shock is what made me fall to the ground and where the girl had kicked me repeatedly, each time punctuating her point.

I shook my head to clear the awful memory.

Thanking Guy for the ride, I held the ice pack the nurse provided me tighter to my face as I slung my bag higher over my shoulder. I saw my father's car in the driveway but noticed that my mother and Estella's vehicle were absent. That at least gave me some relief because my father wouldn't panic as my mother would, and Estella would probably start a search on the leaders of the DyVa group.

Opening the front door, I walked into the cool house, taking my time as I pulled my shoes off and left them near the front door—only flinching slightly when I bent to straighten them. As I was about to drop the bag on the couch, the phone in my bag rang.

Pulling out the phone from the small front zipper pocket, I flipped open the phone case cover to see Dylan called me. Smiling, I immediately answered the call, placing the small phone by my ear.

"Dylan!" I was so excited to hear from him that I couldn't contain the enthusiasm in my voice.

A warm tingle ran down my spine when I heard him chuckle.

"How was your day, sweetheart?"

That was a loaded question. I didn't want to get him worried about the details of the day's events, so I decided to keep the incident a secret. "It was okay. How's filming going?"

"It's going. I miss you, Bree."

A broad smile appeared on my face, making me cringe and suck in a hissed breath. The bruise on my face sent sharp bits of pain all over. Switching the phone to the other ear, I barely heard Dylan asking me what happened—only catching the last part.

"...wrong?"

"Can you repeat that, Dylan? I switched the phone to my other ear, so I think I missed you asking me something."

"I asked you what happened and if something was wrong, Bree."

I sat on the couch. "Nothing you need to worry about. I promise I'm fine."

Again, I missed what he was telling me. The front door slammed against the wall when Estella pushed it open. Her brilliant blue eyes were dark with worry and fury as she made her way inside the house, barely giving me a second to breathe before she hounded me.

"What the hell happened, Bree? Who the hell was this chick that came at you?"

I was about to open my mouth and speak, but Estella wasn't having any of it because she paced the floor in front of me, stopping only to rant.

"Guy called my cell while I was at work and told me that some scary-ass Dylan/Vanessa groupie was attacking you on school grounds. A freaking crazy-ass psycho chick was beating up my little sister, and you didn't bother to call me or tell me?"

I tried to open my mouth again to speak, but Estella silenced me with a hand to my face. "No, I don't want to hear any of it. This crap will not happen again. I will find out what this group is called and make sure to stop it immediately. I have connections, you know. I'm also telling Dad what happened."

"Tell me what?" the man asked from the doorway of his office. I had forgotten for a second that he was home today.

I had also forgotten that Dylan was on the phone. His voice roared from the other end of the line. "What the hell is your sister screaming about? Who attacked you? When did this happen, Bree, and why did you fail to tell me this sooner?"

My eyes turned watery, so I blinked several times to stop myself from crying.

Ready to answer, my father asked again, "What is going on?" as Estella paced the floor like a caged tiger.

The family pulled me in different directions with no chance to explain what happened. Dylan's voice flowed from the phone. My father approached me repeatedly, asking the same question, and Estella related what she heard in her high-pitched voice. The words thrown at me became one huge jumbled mess in my foggy brain, causing me a larger headache than before. The words continually made less sense. My nerves were strung tighter than a guitar, and before I knew it, I was on my feet with tears flowing down my face. I dropped my phone and ran upstairs to my bedroom without saying a word, slamming the door behind me.

I buried my face in the comforter, crying uncontrollably. I didn't ask for this to happen to me today, and I also didn't want Dylan to find out about it. Now, not only did he know what happened from Estella's big mouth, but my father got the rundown from Estella's point of view and not my own. It wasn't that it was much different than what had happened, but I could have explained it less threateningly. I was sure that my parents would be so upset that they would try to stop me from seeing Dylan anymore or become so paranoid that they'd hire me a bodyguard.

I didn't need anyone worrying more than they should. The girl was obsessed and would be treated accordingly. The only reason I wanted to involve my father was that he was a lawyer and could make sure the girl got some much-needed help, especially after the enactment of "Phoebe's Law," an anti-bullying legislation. There were some doors opening and closing downstairs, then footsteps coming toward my door. Wiping the tears from my eyes, I waited until my family tore into me some more.

A light knock on the door made me wipe off the rest of the tears as I called out for whoever it was to enter. I was busy pulling the socks off my feet to see who walked in, but sweet Jesus, I could smell him. My head whipped up as I stared wide-eyed at my boyfriend. Dylan stood by my desk, leaning his hip on the end of it. He had his arms crossed over a full and firm chest as the shirt he wore tightened over the muscles. Jeans sat comfortably on his hips with a broad black belt holding them up. Recently showered, Dylan's long black hair was slicked back away from his gorgeous dark eyes. There wasn't time to regain the air sucked out of my lungs from seeing my handsome man. I jumped from my spot on the bed and into his arms.

Dylan Marcus uncrossed his arms in time to catch me tightly to his chest. I had settled my head on his shoulder with my nose buried in the crook of his neck.

My arms bound around his neck as my legs wrapped around his mid-section. There weren't any words between us, but I felt like the whole stress of the day slowly withered away. Marcus held me tighter as he moved us toward the bed.

Turning around and dropping his weight on it, I didn't bother to let go of him as I cried silent tears into his shirt. Now sitting on the bed with my legs wrapped tightly around him, Dylan soothingly ran his hands up and down my back. My weight rested comfortably on his thighs. For a second, I feared he was merely a figment of my imagination and would disappear the moment I opened my eyes or said something out loud. He should've been in Europe right now, not in my room. The comfort I felt at that moment was what I needed, so I refused to move.

"Sweetheart, I don't know what to do. Would you like to talk?"

I held him tighter to me, afraid I would lose the relief I currently felt by talking right now. I shook my head, worried he would push me to talk about what happened. He didn't. Dylan ran his hands up and down my back in soothing gestures.

"Okay, beautiful. Whenever you're ready."

The understanding he showed me made me cry all over again, and not once did he force me to stop or to let go of him. Dylan sat there on my bed as I let all of my frustrations out on him. He took it all into himself and away from me. After what felt like hours, I finally tore my face from his neck, aware that I had soaked his shirt through with my salty tears. Feeling guilty for ruining his shirt, I pulled back from his chest to search his face as I ran my hands over the moist parts. Dylan's eyes were dark with worry, but I saw so much more buried deeper within their gorgeous depths. He sincerely cared about me. It almost felt as if he begged me not to leave him. If he only knew how in love with him I already was.

With that realization, I was barely able to look at him as I whispered, "Hi."

Dylan's answering smile took my breath away. "Hi," he replied.

I pointed toward his shirt. "I'm sorry about your...."

The words were lost as his mouth covered mine, taking the rest of my frustrations and dialogue with them. He gently pried my lips open with his tongue, tentative, pleading to enter to tease my own. I gladly allowed him entrance, burying my hands in his hair as our mouths danced a rhythm all their own. Pulling slowly away from me, Dylan pressed his lips together and *really* stared at me. He kissed my nose, my cheeks, and forehead before coming back down to the side of my face. The man placed another gentle kiss on the bruise I knew was there.

"You're home."

Dylan kissed me again, lingering on my lips. He whispered against them, "I'm home."

Dylan Marcus Taylor

WHEN I HEARD Estella scream in the background that Brina got attacked by one of my psycho fans, I saw red. I was already on my way to her house, so the news only fueled me to get there faster. Ignoring the speed limit, I rushed over to her home only to knock on the door and receive a lecture from her father on the importance of protecting his daughter.

I already knew that!

If I had to hire a plethora of bodyguards to watch over Bree, I would do so. There was no price limit on how far I'd go to protect my girlfriend. I asked Estella if she knew who attacked Bree, but all she knew was that some classmate named Guy called her and told her the young girl got arrested for assaulting her sister. Unfortunately, they didn't think it would hold because of the girl's age.

Rushing up the stairs toward Bree's room, I had found her sad and bruised. I wanted to run out to the police station myself and file charges against this girl. Even if it meant I had to sue her family for raising such a hell spawn or make a substantial donation to the police department to keep her behind bars long enough to scare the living daylights out of her—then that's what I would do. That damn DyVa group would be the death of me.

The fan club had been operating for about three years now, growing larger and larger as the time went on. They were either the ones causing trouble in my life or sticking their nose in business that was none of theirs. But to see the one woman I cared about on the receiving end of some of my crazed fans upset me on an entirely different level. Brina had seen me and immediately jumped into my arms, wrapping those firm legs around my body.

Then she cried. She cried so much and for so long that my fear for her had tripled. If the only thing I could do for her was let her cry then, I'd willingly stop time for her. I took all of her pain and worries into myself—telling her with my body that I cared about her and would protect her as only I could.

Bree had let it all out.

When she was finally able to, she planted a sweet kiss on my lips and led me to her father's office to explain what happened after school. I wanted to roar to the heavens and seek justice for what she had gone through, but my Bree refused to make matters worse. She insisted that her dad handle getting the family to at least get their daughter some help. That is all she wanted. Any other woman getting that kind of treatment would have expected a whole slew of bodyguards, a private car, and media attention. Not Brina Palace. All my girlfriend wanted was for the crazed DyVa fan to get some psychological help.

"It's no offense to you, Dylan, but it takes someone mentally unstable to go through such risky behavior. I would never do that."

No offense taken.

That's what I enjoyed about her.

Back in her room, she removed some books from the inside of the bag lying on the floor. "I've seen and heard of this stuff on TV, but I would have never thought to be on the receiving end of it."

Bree started working on her class assignments while I watched from my spot on her bed. I was the picture of relaxation as I leaned against her headboard with my legs extended in front of me. With arms folded behind my head, I watched as my girl got comfortable on the bed beside me to do her homework. Bree wore nothing but a pair of stretchy shorts and a body-hugging t-shirt. My heart skipped a beat. Even if she didn't notice my reaction to her, I couldn't help resist telling her over and over again how she made me feel.

Sliding one finger down the back of her exposed calf to her ankle, I relished the feel of her silky skin. I saw her shudder, pleased to see her reaction to my touch.

The one problem was that I was afraid to say anything more to her regarding my feelings. I knew I was falling in love with Brina Palace, but I was more worried she might not see me in the same way. When the press asked me if I was in love with Bree, I only responded that they needed to give our relationship a chance to get there. I was scared about her reaction and glanced over at Bree to see that she was entirely comfortable with that announcement. She didn't flinch or cringe. There were no physical manifestations of her feelings for me at that moment.

I couldn't tell if she was the better actress. Honestly, I was afraid to find out either way. Bree meant so much more to me than I'd led on. Part of that probably had to do with the fact that anytime I got close to someone, it all went to hell in a paper bag. I wasn't ashamed to admit that I was a coward. Losing Bree would break me in more ways than one. But for now, I'd relish seeing her blush as I ran my fingers up and down her leg.

Brina Palace

I WAS LEFT breathless.

Dylan smiled at me again, leaving me at the small two-person bistro table to retrieve our jackets. He had just thoroughly kissed me, taking my lips and branding them with his taste—with his scent. My fingers fluttered toward my swollen lips as the memory of such a kiss brought glorious shards of electricity to run rampant inside of my body. We had a lovely private supper at one of his favorite restaurants in the city after he picked me up after school today. I wished I could have just taken the day to play hooky, but that wasn't the type of person I was. I sucked it up and waited for the school day to be over. Coming home, I had rushed to finish my homework and got ready to go out to supper with Dylan.

We had talked about our favorite movies, foods, places we wished to visit, and all sorts of questions couples asked one another when they were dating. I loved every minute of it. The food was delicious, the company was perfect, and the kiss was…the kiss was magical. There were times when I felt that Dylan's feelings were the same as mine, but then I would remember the conversation with the paparazzi, and I knew it took time for someone to feel out a relationship. Dylan was used to having all types of women vying for his affections. I knew that to be especially suitable for him. Patience was what I needed.

Dylan Marcus Taylor walked back over to our table with natural confidence in each step he took. The man was so handsome I had to study my plate to get my thoughts back together momentarily. Hoping I didn't resemble one of his fans, I smiled when he approached with my jacket. He was animatedly saying something to me, but I couldn't for the life of me figure out what it was as I studied his strong cheekbones covered in that close facial-hair scruff look he sported on his days off. His long hair was slicked back behind his ears, but for one dark strand that refused to stay put. My fingers itched to push it back, so I buried them inside my jacket pockets.

The more he spoke, the more fire lit up his dark eyes from within. The shirt he wore was loose enough not to spark attention, but he couldn't help how it sat on his physique. Dylan's chest was defined through the soft cotton, but I knew from personal experience how intense it was when I was held to that masculine chest several times before.

Dylan leaned into me, kissing me right below my ear. I shivered, a blush adorning my cheeks as it rose from my neck.

"I had a good time tonight," he whispered in that sexy rough voice of his.

He laid his head on my shoulder, staring up at me from his position.

"Me too," was all I could reply.

His eyes dilated as if full of passion. Did he want more from me too?

Clearing my throat, I stared ahead of me as his driver drove the car through the city to get back on the highway. *Passion.* That is what I saw in his eyes. *No.* I shook my head in denial. There was no way that movie star Dylan Taylor felt that way about me. There were so many women all over the world way sexier than me. Dylan had them lining up with their deli ticket stubs in one hand, just waiting to be called up next. Unfortunately, it so happened that my number got called before theirs.

But, it didn't mean my number was the only one he would call. Katy Perry's song *Not like the Movies* played its melody in my head. Was Dylan my fairytale or my actual live prince? I felt a slight pressure on my hand, so I studied how big Dylan's hand was as it encompassed my smaller one in his own. His steady hand protected mine. The action brought warmth into my body.

Darn, I love this man.

Feeling some courage, I turned my head again to see that Dylan's eyes were closed as he breathed deeply from his position on my shoulder. The man had fallen asleep. My heart tightened. Before I even knew what I was doing, I had already leaned in to place a chaste kiss on his eye. I smirked when his thick lashes tickled my still sensitive lips. Dylan's eyes drifted open to stare right back at me. I didn't know what he saw in my eyes but hoped they mirrored his own. He rose from the perch he had on my shoulder, raising one hand to cup the side of my face. My rapid beating heart was so loud; I hoped he couldn't hear it as he leaned in to kiss me, staring intently at my lips the entire time.

He took the kiss deeper, surprised I heard him purr. Or, it could have been me. Right now, I wasn't sure. Our tongues gently played, savoring one another with the promise of more to come. What we had was a silent mutual compromise. His other hand had come around to the back of my head to deepen the kiss. Mine tangled in the silky texture of his hair. I relished the feel as his muscular body pressed itself closer to me. Doubt fluttered in between sucks of air but vanished as the pleasure of our lips sought one another again.

The hand that held the side of my face traveled down to trace the curve of my breast, lower to the dip at my waist, and toward the firmness of my thighs. Dylan lifted me with one hand to straddle his body.

There I sat. I tried to wiggle off of him, embarrassed at our compromising position finally registering in my lust-induced brain. Still, the man had locked his arms around my body—firm hands putting pressure on my back to cease movement. Dylan kissed me again then, taking all of my reserves away. I held him tighter to me for fear I would wake up, and this would all be a dream.

My boyfriend removed his lips from mine. Before I could argue that it was the wrong thing to do, Dylan returned those million-dollar lips to the dip in my neck that quivered with each feverish beat of my heart. My body burned as his lips and tongue traced my collarbone and back up to the side of my neck.

Kiss, suck, nibble, and lick.

Kiss, suck, nibble, and repeatedly lick the different points of my exposed skin. Euphoria was like a drug, and I was addicted to it like a junkie with a fix. One hand remained on my back, kneading the muscles, while the other slid down to my waist, squeezing as we rode our delight in one another. Dylan mumbled endearments in my ear; all the while, his hands did terrific things like slide across the skin of my stomach.

"Mr. Taylor, we have arrived at Miss Palace's home."

Dylan stopped kissing me, bringing me back down to Earth from my trip into Outer Space and the excited prance in the cosmos as I danced merrily from star to star. A quick intake of breath brought him to notice how one would see our position if the driver opened the door. His hands were under my shirt, sitting incredibly still on my lower back. Not as bad as mine, though, which were bunched in his shirt and held still right above his abs.

"Holy crap!" I was about to take his shirt off! I whipped my hands away from Dylan's as if burned by his skin.

Oh my god! I was going to strip Dylan Taylor of his shirt in the back seat of a moving vehicle.

I jumped off him to straighten my clothes and fight with my hair as the door opened on my side. Getting ready to greet the driver and calm the erratic beating of my heart, I belatedly heard what sounded like muffled laughter. Frowning, I turned to look at Dylan, who had a hand covering his mouth. His molten chocolate eyes glimmered in elation.

"Miss Palace?"

Before I got to give him a piece of my mind, the driver held his hand out for me. I took his hand as I slid out of the limo's leather seats. My boyfriend slid out after me, grabbing my hand as we walked to the front door.

"We almost got caught," he teased.

I turned red and stopped walking. In the darkness, I was sure people could spot me by the color pooled in my cheeks.

My eyes searched the vicinity to make sure no one had heard him. "Shh, Dylan. That was…" I trailed off with a hand waving frantically in front of me. "What I did was… What I mean is…."

He leaned into me. "Is the word you looking for… naughty?"

I burned brighter.

"Um."

His finger traced the same collarbone that he had done naughty things to earlier. "I enjoyed tasting you right here."

Dear God, I am going to turn into a puddle of goo.

Taking his hand, I pulled him closer to the front door, trailing a laughing movie star behind me.

"You're incorrigible."

"Only with you, sweetheart."

THIS WAS OUR last day together before Dylan had to fly to New York to film the new scenes for his movie. I had spent a wonderful two days with him, but today we decided to hang out at his house before he had to fly out that night back to The Big Apple. It was my first time coming to his home, so I stood in the foyer, staring in awe at the ample open space. The entrance was extensive, with a chandelier hanging from the top of the vaulted ceilings. From my left, I could see a fully furnished high-tech kitchen in black marble and stainless steel. The floors were all done in cherry hardwood that sparkled as if recently waxed. He had a few paintings on the white walls, but nothing that screamed this was a family home. What I saw was a home modeled after decorating magazines. Cool and aloof.

A staircase wrapped around the house for at least three floors that I could see from my position on the foyer. Dylan walked ahead of me toward the back of the home to see if his Nana was home. I wanted to step into the center of the beautiful room and spin around to take in everything around me, but I contained my giddiness. A small table sat in the foyer with a cordless phone and a picture frame. Gliding toward it, I lifted the silver frame in my hand to study the picture. The room was devoid of anything that screamed homey but this one photo. The photograph had a smiling Dylan Taylor at about six years of age with a dashing older version of him standing to his left, and a woman I assumed was his mother on his right. They seemed so happy together.

"I see you've met my parents."

I turned at the sound of his voice, clutching the frame to my chest. "I-I'm sorry. I didn't mean to pry."

Dylan stood in front of me with an older woman standing behind him. The woman stared at me with calculative curiosity. She measured me from head to toe as if to find me worthy or not of Dylan. Hope filled me. Maybe the woman would see something inside me that's worthy of him.

"A new hussy, Master Taylor?"

Or maybe not.

Dylan shot me a look and then one at his Nana. "Nana!"

The older lady shrugged as if it did not bother her to voice her opinions in such a manner. She floated toward me with her long swirling black skirt swishing between her legs. Facing me, she removed the frame from my hand, wiping it with a rag as she set it back on the table.

I swallowed.

Pouting or withdrawing into myself would not help my case any better than Dylan was at this moment. He stared at his Nana in utter shock.

"Hello, Mrs. Crocker," I began as I extended my

hand in front of me. "My name is Brina Palace. How do you do, ma'am?"

Pumping my hand with a grip, not like an older woman's, I fought hard to keep the smile on my face. It felt like Nana wasn't sure she could trust me because of all the stories circulated of women taking advantage of Dylan's fame or money. I wanted to ease those worries.

"At least you are polite and know some manners."

"Yes, ma'am," I said as we let go. "My parents taught both my sister and me to respect our elders."

She nodded. "Dylan tells me that you are not like the others. Is that true?"

Dylan blushed to his ears as he stared aghast at his Nana. Taking a deep breath, I straightened my posture and spoke to his Nana with all the conviction I could muster. "Mrs. Crocker, I'd like to tell you that I am not like the other women that have hung around Dylan, but I can't."

In my honesty, both of them stared at me aghast.

I put one hand up to stall them from thinking the worst of me before I had a chance to explain. "I assume other women enjoyed his company because of their physical attraction to him. I'm no different. Dylan is beautiful."

He snickered, so my eyes roamed to where he stood. "Well, you are."

I turned back to his Nana. "Women enjoy being treated to restaurants they could never afford before." I remembered going to Dylan's favorite restaurant. I've always wanted to go to that restaurant Brant, but they had a waiting list into next year. "I'm no different. I can't stand here and say I did not like it when he treated me to a five-star restaurant meal. The food was delicious."

If possible, Nana seemed flabbergasted. "Also, I am sure other women enjoy the changes in people's characters around them when they find out who they are dating. Well, Mrs. Crocker, I'm no different."

She was about to say something, but I cut her off. "However, my being with Dylan is not in the same context as those other women. I think Dylan is gorgeous, but his beauty isn't what attracted me in the first place. We didn't know what each other looked like as our feelings grew for one another through text. Yes, I enjoy going out to restaurants, but it isn't because Dylan is paying for a meal that costs more than what I make in a year." I turned to Dylan. "Which I still think is ridiculous, by the way."

Seeing Dylan's smile made me continue. "I love to eat. It doesn't matter if he takes me to Papa Ginos or a restaurant on Boylston Street. Food is yummy anywhere. It just so happened that his particular tastes are more refined than my own. Now, in regards to people changing their tune around me because I'm the girlfriend of a famous movie star—" I shrugged.

"I'm used to being a loner. Yes, it's nice that I have more people saying hi to me as I walk the school halls, but I'm not under any illusions to obtain an entourage. I like my social status. Because of Dylan, my sister and I have a better relationship now. So in answer to your question, Mrs. Crocker, I *am* like the other women around Dylan, but the only difference between them and me is that my feelings for him are genuine. They weren't created because of his material possessions.

My feelings were built upon trust the longer we spoke, depended on one another, and have come to care for one another through a simple form of technology a lot of us take for granted these days."

Dylan Marcus Taylor walked around his Nana and toward me. Taking my small hands in his, he leaned in and placed a quick kiss on my lips. I was trembling inside. Hopefully, his Nana wouldn't dismiss me as another one of his crazy exes. And that all my ramblings haven't made matters worse between the woman Dylan considered a mother and the woman he claimed as his girlfriend.

"Well, I'll be, young lady. I see now why my Dylan fancies you. I've seen the smile you put on his face, Miss Palace. So long as you keep that particular smile on his face, you and I have no qualms with one another." She extended her hand. "It was a pleasure meeting you."

Smiling, I shook hands one last time with Dorothea Crocker, waving goodbye as the woman patted Dylan on the shoulder and walked back into the kitchen.

Phew.

Disaster averted.

For now.

Dylan Marcus Taylor

I COULDN'T BELIEVE Bree had that much courage built within her. We took a moment to tour the inside of my house, but as she glanced around in awe, all I could do was the same when I looked at her. Brina was so beautiful and fitting for me. I didn't care much for the interior of this house. I had hired an interior decorator to make it look fancy and tasteful, but the only place I considered my own within the vast interior was my room.

Taking her by the hand, I reached the large Mahogany double doors that led into my bedroom. I wasn't worried she'd find clothes on the floor or an unmade bed. Nana was so good at her job that I never feared bringing a guest to my room or giving them an eyeful of my laziness.

One thing I never did was clean anything. For one, Dorothea never allowed me to do so, and second because I was always so tired from my projects and different jobs. Not everyone was perfect—not even me. I led my girlfriend into the bedroom and closed the door behind me to give us some privacy. Brina walked into the room and laughed.

"I was worried for a bit that your personal space would be so much like the cold, detached interior of the rest of the house."

I stared at my room again through her eyes.

Brina squealed when she spotted Charlie on my bed. "Can I pet him?"

I nodded and watched as my girlfriend went over to Charlie and cooed over him. Other girls I'd introduced to Charlie always gave him a wide berth. He was a loving dog. Sometimes a little too friendly. He enjoyed lapping my dates with his drool kisses, and they hated it. Brina didn't. I saw my dog's tail wag and his snout sniff her face as Charlie placed long wet kisses on it.

"I'm getting jealous," I joked.

She smiled at me and rubbed Charlie's fur. "You should. He's so cute!"

Charlie sucked up all of the attention. I did feel a little bit jealous because I wanted all her focus on me and me only. I called for Charlie and watched the dog jump down from my high bed and let him out of the room.

"Aw, why did you send him away?"

I closed the door and ran toward her. Brina squealed again and braced for me to lift her into my arms and throw her on my bed. She laughed when she landed on the plush comforter and pillows.

"He, young lady, needs to potty. You need to come here."

I inched nearer to her and enjoyed seeing her jade eyes brighten. She moved a little bit closer to me but made no move to do anything else. I leaned into her face, but she inched back. Her rejection shocked me. I didn't mean to do anything she didn't want to do.

"You're moving away from me? I'm sorry."

She giggled. "My face is covered in dog drool, dummy. It's not you."

I sat up on the bed with a smile I couldn't fake. Brina made me feel like a teenage boy. I grabbed her by the ankles and dragged her closer to me, then leaned over her and watched as she blinked several times. Her face got pink, and when she bit her lips, I couldn't help but bend down to grab her lips with my own.

Dog drool forgotten.

I pressed my body to hers and kissed her senselessly. She had whipped her arm around one side and grabbed hold of my shirt between her tiny fingers. The other buried into my hair, pressing me down tighter. I shifted her leg and nestled between them. The heat radiating from both our bodies drove me mad with lust.

Not just lust. I loved Bree.

Brina had slipped her hand inside of my shirt and slid it up higher. I helped by pulling it off my body and tossing it across the room. She ran her fingers all over my exposed skin and then dug her nails into the flesh of my back to pull me closer to her. I was savoring her neck and running my hand underneath her shirt as her fingers continued their perusal of my body. Brina dropped her hands from my body, causing goosebumps to litter my flesh. She grabbed the hem of her shirt and pulled it over her head in one swift move. Bree lay on my bed in her bra.

My heart beat furiously behind my ribcage. Brina was more beautiful to me in her vulnerable state than ever before. I leaned down and nipped her collarbone with my teeth. She had run one hand down my belly and maneuvered the button that held my jeans up. I ran my hand down the side of her body as she wrapped her leg around mine. My mind went blank. I gingerly pulled down one strap of her bra, careful not to expose her too quickly. I kissed the barren spot.

She was about to place her hand inside the waistband of my jeans when my door slammed open, and my cousin hollered that he had arrived. I heard several screams at once. Me yelling at June to leave and Bree's as she fled to my bathroom—the moment broken. I sat on the bed and watched my cousin's beet-red face slowly close the door behind him. I punched the bed, but not because I was mad. I wasn't angry that June had interrupted us. Admittedly, I was glad he did. Bree wasn't ready emotionally for a physical relationship, even though her body most definitely was. I wouldn't let her make that kind of decision under the heat of the moment.

Not her.

Not my Bree.

I slid off of the bed, grabbing my shirt and tossing it

back on. Taking a look around, I noticed that Bree had already taken her shirt with her. Buttoning my pants, I knocked on the door of the bathroom.

"Sweetheart, are you alright?"

Her voice sounded muffled. "Uh, yeah."

"Can I come in?"

She was silent for a moment and then opened the door. "I'm sorry," she said.

I smiled and kissed her on the lips. "Nothing you should be sorry for."

Bree looked around me and into the room. Noticing that June was nowhere around, she asked me, "Did he see anything?"

"I was covering your body; I'm sure he didn't see you."

She blanched. "B-but, I ran from the bed and into the bathroom. He was still in the room!"

I laughed. "Baby, June was so embarrassed he did not pay any attention to what you were doing."

"Are you sure?"

I laughed again, wiping a tear from her eye. "Bree, I promise you. It'll be okay."

She nodded.

I kissed her on the lips once more, and she kissed me back ever so fiercely. I could feel my entire body go hot in the most compelling manner. With nothing else on my mind but her, I pinned her body against the bathroom wall and lifted her into my arms. She kissed me deeper, breathing into my mouth so hot and heavy that I couldn't resist her.

She pulled her mouth from mine. "Dylan, I..."

I couldn't let her finish. If she told me she loved me,

then I'd make love to her right now and get mad at myself later. And if she told me she didn't want to go through with this, I'd go crazy also. It was better if I didn't know.

"Sweetheart, I think we should take deep breaths right now. June's probably still waiting to talk to me."

She blinked rapidly and nodded. "Oh, uh, yeah. Of course."

I'm an igit.

Brina Palace

WITH DYLAN IN New York finishing up the filming of his movie, I focused on finishing the last days of my junior year in high school. I spoke to Mable's original owner, Reba, and am working off the dress by operating the cash register and helping circulate the products in the antique store. If I wasn't doing something for school or talking to my busy boyfriend, I was working at Reba's and daydreaming about the almost moment in Dylan's bedroom. I wanted it, but after June barged in, Dylan put some distance between us and physically kept me at arm's length. We hadn't talked about it again since that day. Dylan called me on his breaks and sent me messages every night before going to bed.

He worked hard and had no time to spare for us. I didn't push him. Dylan was a great actor and an excellent role model, not just because of his dedication to his roles and morals. The one thing I would never do is become one of those girls that monopolized all his time. I would have to settle for his text messages, occasional phone and video calls, and a couple of shots here and there by different media outlets. I finished closing up for the night. As I walked home, my phone went off in my pocket.

I stopped walking to write back.

I stared at the time on the phone and realized that

it was a little past ten at night. Dylan was probably on break and only had a few minutes to text me before he had to run back to do his job. I turned on a music app on my phone, hiding the earphones underneath my loose hair. The phone in hand, I stuffed my hands into the pockets of my mom jeans and walked back home. Things were finally going right in my world. My class-mates backed off and took me more seriously. I'd made a great friend in Guy and had an excellent sister in Estella. With my sister getting ready to graduate and head off to college, I thought about how things would be without her around. My phone went off again.

I hoped Dylan had some time off before another job to spend time with me. He wanted to hang out over the summer, but as much as I wanted that, I didn't want him to have any issue with his manager, agent, law-yer, drill sergeant—the titles that woman wore were many. I was going to work a lot over the summer too, but I wanted at least one long weekend with my love before my senior year began, and things got crazier for both him and me. I contemplated this and many other things before reaching my home and coming to a dead stop. A shiny, black SUV was parked in front of my house. I ran toward the car, hoping it was Dylan.

The door opened, and the first thing I noticed was a dazzling stiletto heel touch down on the pavement. I stopped running. The door closed, and standing in front of me was the last person I'd ever thought to see. Vanessa Dallas tipped her head to one side and winked. My short stature and dry locks were nothing compared to her tall height and long flowing blonde hair. The scent of her perfume reached the spot where my shoes were rooted. I didn't compare to this alluring woman standing before me. Vanessa was perfectly coifed and ready for the runaway, even in a pair of skinny jeans and a loose blouse.

"Hello, Brina Palace."

I couldn't help but study my surroundings. Vanessa obviously addressed me, but I was still unsure as to why. "Uh, I'm rather surprised to see you again, Miss Dallas."

Vanessa put her hand to her chin and stared up at the dark sky. "Hm, I don't recall ever meeting you before." She looked back at me. "Have we met before now?"

I was just reminded how incredibly unimportant I was to the world of the elite. "Uh, yes, Miss Dallas. We met at the event for the Sheik unveiling."

She smiled and giggled. "Ah, I had met so many

people that day that I can't quite remember." She took a step to the side and gestured to her vehicle. "Mind if we talk more inside?"

There were plenty of times before where I would imagine a scenario just like this one. Never in my wildest dreams had I ever believed that I'd be dating a famous actor, have fallen in love with him, and have prominent people surprise me at my home. I nodded and walked toward the open car door, sliding in before Vanessa and to the other side. Vanessa sidled up next to me and closed the door.

"Well then…"

Dylan Marcus Taylor

I ACHED EVERYWHERE and was beyond tired. We were wrapping up the last scene, so everyone ran to do other things on our quick break. I wanted to walk over to my camper and grab my cell phone, but I was too tired to walk farther than my chair to take a quick ten-minute nap. I had barely plopped into my chair before an unwelcome voice came around the corner. I lifted one eye open as my head rested on my chin. Vanessa's golden waves came into view. She smiled at me.

"You look so exhausted, darling."

I was in and out of consciousness, but I heard her calling out to some of the assistants as if she was in control. It was better not even to bother paying her any attention. I tuned her out and fell asleep. Behind my eyelids, I could see Brina running toward me. I felt her run her fingers through my hair, and I smiled. Bree always ran her fingers through my hair. Whenever we were near one another, she always had her fingers buried deep in my hair and I enjoyed every minute of it.

"Darling, wake up. They're about to go back out there, and makeup needs to powder you before you do."

The words and the person they came from had me bolting up from my precarious position. I noticed that Vanessa had laid my head on her lap and had been caressing my head as I slept. The chair I had sat on fell back from the strength of my actions. I glared at Vanessa and around me to all of the people milling about getting their jobs done. Some of the females I noticed had blushes on their faces, while others watched me with distaste.

What the hell just happened?

"Vanessa, I don't know why the hell I was on your lap, but I'd appreciate it if you showed my girlfriend and me some respect."

Vanessa laughed as makeup made its way toward me. One girl grabbed the chair from the floor while the other ushered me back into it. They were patting my face down and fixed my hair as Vanessa spoke.

"Well, I came to give you some great news." She stood in front of me as I sat in the chair, getting fixed up for the final scene. "Do you remember that investor we met at your cousin's event?"

I only stared.

"Okay, well, he just called and sent an amazing

script that would solidify our statures as amazing actors. The script is so great that I foresee a lot more than just Golden Globes and Oscar's. Trust me on this, Dylan."

She handed me the script. I took it and nodded at my makeup artist when she told me she finished. Getting up, I placed the writing on the seat.

"I'll look it over later."

Vanessa whipped her hair to one side and smiled coquettishly. "Call me when you realize its greatness, and I'll explain more."

The final scenes had gone off without a hitch. Everyone had applauded and congratulated one another on a job well done. I spent the flight back to my home reading the script Vanessa had brought me. In reality, I couldn't put it down. The movie explored the human soul—the power of love through a time of madness and solitude and the battle of war reigning its supremacy over the unwilling people. Like my first film about the soldier, I wanted to play a role that took me entirely out of my comfort zone. The movie I currently wrapped up was nothing compared to what this movie could do for my career.

I needed to know more and couldn't wait to get off the plane to call Vanessa. When she answered the phone, her first words were, "I knew you'd devour it as I did."

I leaned back in my seat and stared at the clouds gliding by me. "I don't usually agree with you, but this script is pure genius."

"Exactly what I thought myself."

I smelled a "but" coming. "What's the catch, Vanessa?"

She laughed. "No catch, Dylan. He wants you and me as the leads, and filming will start next week."

Next week.

Any other time I would've jumped right on it, but this time I had to second-guess myself. I didn't want to get right back to work when I just came out of it. With the story's setting, I was sure that I would be placed in remote locations with barely any signal to no signal whatsoever. *Damn.* I could be gone for long weeks and months on end without a break. It's not right to put Brina in that kind of position. We would miss one another far too much. I'd be unfocused for sure. Plus, I wanted a vacation, and I promised to take her on one. The pain I felt missing out on this once-in-a-lifetime role was less than the pain I'd feel leaving Brina for such a long time.

Clearing my throat, I closed the window shade beside me. Watching the gray clouds right now made me feel even more somber. "I…" I took a deep breath. "I can't take the role."

She was silent for a second before ripping into me. "Are you crazy? This is the best role you have ever come across! Please don't tell me you are basing this rejection because of your relationship with that girl?"

"You wouldn't understand. I've fallen in love, Vanessa." I sighed and shook my head even though I knew Vanessa couldn't see me.

Vanessa went silent once more, but this time, when she came back on the line, her voice was much softer than before. "If she cares for you, she'll understand. I… I've gotta go."

She hung up the phone without giving me a chance to say anything else. I placed my cellphone on the empty seat beside me. I thought about the consequences of declining that movie offer, but my pain at being away from Brina for such a lengthy amount of time hurt a lot more. A project of this magnitude would take years to complete. Besides, I was sure other offers would eventually come my way. *Yes,* other offers would come. For right now, I would enjoy my time off with the woman I fell in love with.

More offers would come.

I was sure of it.

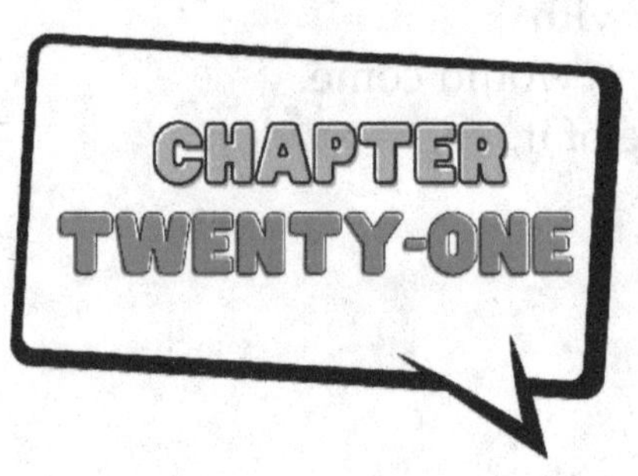

Brina Palace

THE CLASS HAD ended for the day, and I couldn't be happier. These were the last few moments of my courses, and I couldn't afford to get bad grades. Unfortunately, I couldn't focus, and it was only going downhill. Articles upon articles had come out the day before with pictures of Dylan as he lay on Vanessa's lap in New York. He had a special smile he only reserved for me on his face that almost broke my heart in two. But, I knew that Vanessa set it up as an excuse for me to leave Dylan.

My classmates murmured behind my back, and I couldn't help but listen in on their conversations. I was a homewrecker because Vanessa and Dylan were together before I came into the picture, or the superstar used me to heighten his exemplary image.

I walked to my locker. When I got there, I put some books back inside and pulled out my backpack. I checked my phone and saw I had three missed texts. I ignored them. I sighed once more. Since the incident, Dylan had called and texted me. Unfortunately, I needed to ignore the messages and pull away from him. It was all part of the plan. Being with me would only hold him back, and I couldn't live with myself if that happened.

I thumbed through the messages.

Is he heading over to get me? Get me from where?

My heart skipped a beat. Was Dylan here at the school waiting for me? Any other day I'd be beyond giddy. The only thing I accomplished right now was trying to hold back bile. I saw my sister a few feet away with the same look I was sure was on my face. I walked up to her, trying to hold back the tears in my eyes.

Estella sighed. "Are you sure you need to do this? There might be other ways."

I nodded but said nothing.

"He's outside. Kids are surrounding his car, but he's standing there as if they didn't exist. He's a little bit pissed off, and I'm sure it's because you have been ignoring him. No man likes to be kept on read."

I looked toward the doors we were about to walk out of as I mumbled, "He's never ignored his fans like that before."

My eyes fluttered closed as I remembered the night

Vanessa Dallas visited my home.

"So, um, to what do I owe this visit Miss Dallas?"

The beautiful actress smiled at me as she blinked prettily. It reminded me how imperfect I was compared to her. She took a dainty finger to a strand of her hair, sweeping it over her ear as if in a romance novel—the move deliberate and endearing. Something I could never pull off myself.

"Here, take a look through this."

Vanessa handed me a wad of papers clipped together. The booklet had been flipped through several times. There were colored post-its in-between the pages and creases where it had been folded constantly and dog-eared. I flipped through it, page by page, finally registering what these papers were meant to convey.

"Is this a new script?"

She smiled again. "Oh, darling, you are quite perceptive."

I ignored the underlining bit of sarcasm weaved in the remark. "Why are you showing this to me?" I asked, even though I already knew the answer.

"Are you truly in love with Dylan?"

This was not what I expected her to say. "Um, of course I am."

She turned to face me. "I don't believe you are."

I shook my head in denial. What does she know?

"You can't sit here and tell me you know exactly what I'm feeling. Pardon my saying so, but you don't even know me or Dylan for that matter."

Her finger moved to place the strand back behind her ear. "Haven't you ever noticed a trend in a majority of his movies, Brina Palace?"

I shrugged. "What do you mean?"

"Every woman gave him up in some form or another in those movies so that he could be happy and not regretful of his choices."

My head spun. "S-spell it out for me," I managed to say through clenched teeth.

She giggled. "I'm telling you to break up with him."

My sister's last comment and Vanessa's conversation days before had finally caused the tears to trickle down my face. Estella quickly swiped at them so others wouldn't see it. I was already screwing up that man's life. I needed to realize he didn't belong to me. He belonged to everyone. All of his adoring fans and clients. Not the fantastical whims of a teenage girl who so happened to have found his phone in a dark theater one night and exchanged messages with him. I took a deep breath for courage and walked away from my sister to put the plan into motion.

Outside, I could easily spot Dylan standing like a god against the hood of his Audi. My sister was right when she told me he seemed pissed off. Dylan had ignored the fans' efforts for an autograph or a picture. I inhaled some of the fresh springtime air and walked toward his car. Right now, I needed all the help I could get. He spotted me and uncrossed his legs. His sunglasses hid his eyes, so I couldn't tell what he was thinking. I knew what he felt if his posture was anything to go by. When I got closer, he held the passenger door open for me and assisted me inside. My classmates moved away from the car as if sensing the impending doom that was about to implode.

He got inside the car and turned on the vehicle. Dylan hadn't yet said anything to me. I slid my bag on the floor between my legs, knowing full well that inside it was the bait Vanessa set for me.

Our conversation came back to mind.

"What in the world are you talking about? I could never break up with him, especially not because you're telling me to," I replied as confident as I could and handed the papers back to her.

"This script is a once-in-a-lifetime opportunity for Dylan. It is the movie that will change his entire career for the better. The one movie that will give him what he's worked his entire life for. Are you really able to sit there and smugly tell me that you won't break up with him?"

Her words squeezed their way from my brain and into my heart. "B-but why would I have to break up with him?

She sighed as if the answer was obvious to everyone but me. "You are truly so blind?"

I didn't answer.

"Dylan will give up this role for you. Do you think you are worth it?"

Why would he give this role up for me? I couldn't understand anything that she was saying, but losing Dylan wasn't in the cards for me. "I wouldn't let him give it up."

She didn't even wait for me to finish the rest of my thoughts before she said, "You already have." Vanessa lifted the manuscript. "The movie is overseas and you wouldn't see or speak to each other for a long time. I mean long. Years even. He made the decision to reject this movie the moment he made the decision to date you." She threw the papers into my lap. "How incredibly selfish you are to do this to the person you claim to love."

My knee shook. I used my hand to help ease the nerves, but my efforts were futile. Dylan steered us away from the school and toward the highway. I didn't know where we were going, but I couldn't do this if we weren't on my home turf.

"My parents aren't home. Let's talk there."

He nodded and turned the car toward my street instead. My heart hammered behind my chest. I took deep breaths but still felt like I was about to pass out. We made it to my house. He parked in the driveway. I grabbed my bag and took the seatbelt off. I ran out of the car before he got around to opening the door for me. He would follow behind me toward the front door, so I didn't bother checking to see if he accompanied me. I unlocked the door and walked inside.

"Y-you want something to drink?"

He shook his head. Instead, he opted for sitting down on our couch.

Dylan sat in front of me with his elbows resting on his knees and his head in his hands. I stood awkwardly in front of him, trying to control the flurry of tears threatening to fall. My nerves challenged me to sit down or lock myself in my room and never come out. I wasn't a liar and didn't know if I could accomplish what I had set out to do. I didn't want to be the reason why his world changed for the worse. I couldn't be the selfish person Vanessa made me out to be. He was the most important man in the world to me besides my father. Taking a deep breath of air once more, I promised myself not to screw this up.

"Listen, I can't do this."

Dylan's head shot up. He had taken off his sunglasses and now studied me with eyes full of tortured pain. "What in the hell are you talking about? Can't do what?"

I flinched but stood my ground. He had a right to be upset with me. I had been ignoring his calls and messages ever since I spoke to Vanessa. I couldn't take this role away from him.

The only thing I had told him the day before when he insisted on speaking to me was that "I was busy and didn't have time to deal with his excuses." He was rightfully mad. Still, when he wrote me and told me he would spend more time with me from now on, I knew it meant he had or was going to decline the offer for that movie Vanessa had shown me.

When she called me out inside the limo all I could do was cry. *Vanessa Dallas shoved a box of tissues on my lap, on top of the manuscript. I couldn't control the tears as they fell down my face. The drops fell on the cover of the script, penetrating into the paper intrusively. Kind of like me with Dylan Marcus. I tore into his private life only caring of my own wants and needs.*

"Think of the man you love, Brina Palace," she said as I wiped the tears from my face with a tissue. "His entire career would be ruined. The promise he made his parents before they died..."

My eyes shot up. "I-I would n-never," I pleaded one last time.

"I already told you. You already have. He gave up this role before it was even handed to him. If he doesn't do it, he'll be blacklisted in the industry. The media will utterly admonish his behavior. He'll lose all his sponsors. Do you really want to be the reason he loses it all?

I didn't want to be that reason.

Now I stood in front of the man I loved and had to

encourage him to do what he was meant to do without any regrets. Even if we agreed to do this and take the distance from one another, I knew we would both be utterly miserable. Vanessa told me that the only way this would work is if I made him hate me. That way, if he ever felt the urge to miss me, he would be angry instead and use that energy toward his work. I decided to sit down on the couch across from him.

"Dylan, I believed you the first time you told me there was nothing between you and Vanessa. What's that saying? Fool me once shame on you, fool me twice…."

"That's crap, Brina!"

I almost flinched again but stood my ground this time. "Stop trying to intimidate me!"

Dylan almost reared back in shock. "Sweetheart, listen, I'm so—"

"No," I yelled.

My eyes closed, pressure building behind them. "I told you when I first found your phone that I'm tired of the bullies. I'm tired of being treated like I don't matter." I got up from my seat, and Dylan jumped up from his. "You can't talk your way out of this one."

I walked toward my bag and pulled out the picture of Dylan smiling comfortably in Vanessa's lap to punctuate my point. This picture was the reason I'd break up with him. Throwing it on the coffee table in front of us, I yelled, "This picture says a lot more than I needed to know."

Dylan ran a hand through his hair. "Bree, nothing is going on between Vanessa and me. I promise you!"

I shook my head and put a hand up to keep him

away when he tried to approach me. "I can't do this anymore."

My good-looking man shook his head before I could even finish my statement. My eyes only watched him react, and it felt as if my entire world would break. He was so beautiful. Whether he smiled or ached, no one could take that away from him.

"Don't do this to me, Bree." He came toward me anyway. My hand landed on his chest, right above his heart. "Feel my heartbeat. It beats for you and you only." He held the hand to his chest. "Brina, I lo—"

I screamed and put my hands on my ears like a petulant child. If I let Dylan go further, then the plan would fail. I knew that if he said he "loved me," then I couldn't go through with this at all. If I pretended that he didn't, then this wouldn't be as hard as it could be.

"Please, I can't do this anymore. I'm tired of being second best." I made a fist, using my nails to cut into the palm of my skin. It was better that I felt pain else-where than in my heart.

"I want a guy who isn't recognized by the entire world." I could see him processing my words as his eyes narrowed. "Being with you wasn't the same as being with one of your characters would have been. I was living under the illusion that you were them when you were not. You're not the guy I want. Honestly, I fell for Dylan Taylor, the guy in the movies. I'm sorry, but I don't feel the same about Marcus."

That had done it.

I saw the moment his heart had broken, and his eyes lost all of their will to fight. Fat tears ran down my face as I watched him struggle with tears of his own. His fingers shook. He didn't even face me, only stared at the floor at his feet. I wanted to run to him and console him. I wanted to wrap him in my arms and beg forgiveness. I wanted to tell him I was lying and couldn't live without him, but I didn't. Dylan grabbed his keys from the coffee table and straightened.

"Wow, I guess you've made yourself clear then." He ran his hand to push his hair away from his face. "I'll leave you be. No girl had ever made herself any clearer." Dylan walked toward the door. "I wish you the best."

He opened the door, closing it quietly behind him.

I watched him walk out of the door and out of my life. My legs could no longer support my weight, dropping me to the floor as I cried. My body shook from the unbearable pain. I sobbed more than I ever had in my entire life—more than I thought was possible. The wails were so loud it grained on my ears. I felt numb all over. My whole life, I prided myself on my honesty. Now I was the biggest, most disloyal person in the world and a liar to boot.

In my mind, I deserved this pain and more. For the rest of my life, I would live with the knowledge that I had just broken my true love's heart. I didn't know how long I wept before I felt warm arms wrap around my quivering form. My hands rubbed at the tears that wouldn't stop falling. Estella stood in front of me with pity on her face. Although she wasn't onboard with the idea, she supported me anyway. I could hear her speak, but no words penetrated my mind. My sister lifted me off the floor. I tried to remain upright, but my legs were numb and my knees weak. Each time I took a step, I missed or dropped to the floor before she ushered me into my room and laid me on the bed. My eyes roamed the walls of my room, but I could not see a thing through the tears.

Please, God, let me have made the right decision.

"Brina?"

I examined my sister's silhouette.

"I know it hurts more than you can bear right now, but I promise you that time will heal your wounds."

I didn't want to acknowledge that Estella was right. Eventually, it wouldn't hurt as much. I turned to stare at nothing again and then chose instead to close my eyes. The weight on the bed shifted. Estella had left my room, so I decided to keep my eyes shut. I needed to make the pain go away.

I needed the pain to disappear for the rest of my life.

Dylan Marcus Taylor

THE LOUD EXPLOSIONS rang behind me. I ran farther away with the woman my character loved trailing behind me. The moment we moved past the camera angle we were using to film this scene, I dropped Vanessa's hand and walked away from her. The director yelled cut, and the crew cheered. We'd been shooting on an island far off the Philippine Islands and Pacific coast for quite a few months now. My schedule was jam-packed with things I needed to accomplish. I made damn sure Robin had me busy for every second of my day.

"Are you going to continue staying mad at me?"

Her voice came from behind me, and the sound grated on my ears. I turned around so quickly she was unprepared and almost fell back. "Don't get it twisted, Vanessa. Just because I'm a great actor and can fool everyone on the screen into thinking you mean the world to me, it doesn't mean I give a *real* damn about you."

I saw her swallow and the color of her face visibly drain. For a second, I felt terrible about what I said, but then my stubborn side kicked in, and I remembered what she had done to me.

"I get you are still mad about the tabloid thing, but that was months ago, and for us, that means years already. You need to get over it."

My feet took me two steps closer to her before I even realized what they were doing. If she weren't a female, I would have bashed her already. "Get over it? If it weren't for you, Brina and I wouldn't have split up the way we did. We..."

"We what, Dylan? If it weren't me, then it would be some other female. Did she specifically tell you that I'm the issue here?"

I had never really thought about it, but Vanessa was right. Brina never told me that Vanessa was the issue. I was the issue. I wasn't the man she thought I was and that was my fault. She was fascinated with the idea of the star, not the actual person. Brina wanted the fairy-tale where I would move heaven and Earth for her, and we'd live happily ever after like in my movies. I wasn't that man. I had my flaws like any normal human being, and my work sometimes caused more trouble than was necessary. Celebrity life would always put her in the limelight. The paparazzi and crazed fans would mistreat her.

Vanessa was right.

The issue wasn't her; it was me.

Being a superstar meant I couldn't have a regular life. She grew up in a world that was simple, with two loving parents, and things she could do in a moment's notice. I had my every day planned out for me—from the clothes I wore to the dates I'd have. The only decision I made for myself was to date Bree, and even then I was a wicked fool to pull her into a world she wasn't from. Our breakup wasn't Vanessa's fault. Our breakup was all on me.

I couldn't reverse time. My time as a youth was over. Bree was only really starting hers. I'd never belong there.

I wanted to run my hands through my hair, but it was no longer there. The character in the story had a military-type haircut, so I had to lose the long locks Brina loved so much. I took off the beret I wore and used it to cover my face. I didn't want anyone to see how much pain I still felt from our breakup. We never said anything to anyone, nor did my publicists confirm the media's speculations about us breaking up.

I didn't want to prove to the entire world that we weren't together anymore. When someone asked my cousin about the status of our relationship, he had told the reporters that from what he knew, we were still head over heels for one another. June knew the truth already, but he, too, didn't accept it to be fact.

My assistant came over with a water bottle. I took

a swig and scanned the scene I recorded through a set of monitors. The director was avid about ensuring that the actors and camera crew did everything right before moving on to the next scene. I enjoyed filming this movie and thought that maybe I was supposed to do it. That maybe our breakup was for something worthwhile.

Thinking about her again made my heart ache. I threw the beret on the table behind me and got up from my chair. They called the extras in for some scenes in the jungle. I probably had another ten minutes before they would call me in for my next segment. It was best to walk over to the costume artist to grab my next set of clothes. Vanessa was already in there getting into her outfit.

It wasn't the first time I had seen her semi-nude. To me, she appeared like anyone else. She didn't make my blood boil as Brina did.

That night in my home when she had taken her shirt off was more than enough to make me go mad. Vanessa was every man's dream come true. She stared up at me as the assistant buttoned up the back of her dress. I could only see right through her. Since the breakup, I saw nothing and no one anymore. I unbuttoned my worn jacket to get the new one on. Someone handed me my coat.

"I'm sorry, Dylan."

Vanessa walked out of the trailer's door. I wondered what she had to be sorry about, but I couldn't muster up the energy to care. I got my new pants on, jacket, and shiny new boots. Once done, I walked back out of the trailer and toward the next scene I would be filming.

If I wanted to help this movie succeed, then I would have to put Brina in the back of my mind.

Or at least, I could try.

There was still a lot of filming to do. The next few months would be grueling.

I had to try.

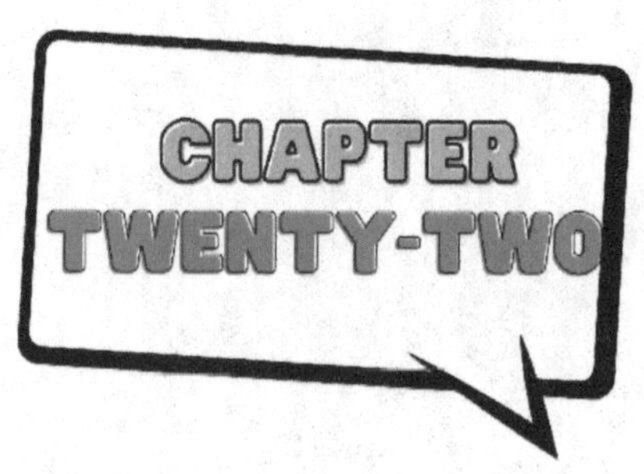

Brina Palace

"THANK YOU FOR shopping with us! Have a good night!"

It was almost closing time, so this would be the last person to visit the shop tonight. Reba was in the backroom fishing up some new merchandise. I walked toward the door and locked it. We had another ten minutes before closing, but the town was dead; barely anyone roamed the streets. I walked over to the cashier's box and counted the money for close-out. Reba came out of the back and turned on the small flat screen she had on the counter.

295

Gossip Weekly played in the background. I saw Penelope wriggle around in a skimpy skirt and an off-the-shoulder blouse. I shook my head. The host always wore skirts when she had male guests on the show. I had watched this show for so long I already knew the woman's method of operating.

I counted the last amount of change and wrote everything down in my currency log as Reba hummed to the show's theme song. Once the money was inside a deposit bag, I set it to the side. The crowd cheered. I watched as Juniel Taylor-Lemore walked on the stage and gave Penelope a hug and a kiss on the cheek. Reba put up the volume on the TV.

"Welcome back to the show Juniel!"

He smiled and waved to the crowd. "It's so great to be here again."

She flirtatiously patted his hand as she leaned in and giggled. "We were sad to hear that your relationship with the beautiful model Francesca Petra came to an end."

"Unfortunately, it was inevitable." June didn't show if it hurt him to talk about it. "She was swamped, and so was I. It wouldn't be fair to one another to continue allowing the roots of a relationship to grow when there wasn't a solid foundation to hold a blossoming tree."

The crowd shouted their sympathies. Penelope wiped a fake tear from her eye.

"Speaking of break-ups, the news going around is that Dylan and his girlfriend have broken up as well."

June smiled as he shook his head. "My cousin's life is private, Ms. Samson. However, I will tell you what I have told everyone that has asked me about them.

As far as I know, they are still head over heels for one another."

My heart skipped a beat. Was June trying to tell me something? Did Dylan still care about me? Did our break-up still hurt him, or did he hold out for a miracle as I did? I would follow him around on the news and tabloids as often as I could. In the last few months, he was quiet because of the movie he filmed overseas. When he had a break, the reporters would find him with a plastic woman pressed to his side at one club or another. The photos never showed him doing anything but sitting next to her. Dylan didn't look at them, and he didn't touch them. The reporters tried their very best to catch him with another woman, but he never gave them a solid reason to think he was single again.

Some reporters had come up to me, and I, too, refused to say anything about it. My reason was that I couldn't admit to myself and the world around us that we were no longer an item. I harbored fantasies that he would come back to me, but then I'd be admitting that I only cared about the illusion of his character versus the man he indeed was. I didn't want the lie I gave him to be accurate. He didn't deserve that, and I was already plenty wrong for him. June had answered another question Penelope asked him. I paid attention to the screen again.

"So, are you going to come out with another fragrance? Sheik is doing incredibly well."

He shifted in his chair. "My scientists and I are working hard on bringing the people quality over quantity."

I remembered back to the moment June had walked

in on my in-depth make-out session with his cousin. It made me grin, thinking that the man must have been so embarrassed. More so than I had been. I watched as Reba walked back to the storage room. Gossip Weekly went into a commercial break, so I changed the channel, leaving it on a black and white movie. The romance on screen made me sick to watch. Reba walked in just as I turned the TV back off.

"What were ya watching?"

I handed Reba the deposit bag and grabbed my purse from underneath the counter. "I was watching a little bit of some black and white movie. I got everything ready for deposits tomorrow. The register has the morning take already in it, and the card machine was closed out for the night. Don't forget to put the tray in the safe."

Reba scoffed. "I've been doing this a long time before you, missy."

I had begun to care for Reba like family. I had been working with her for almost half a year now and loved the sassy older woman. It started as a way to pay her back for Mabel, but turned into a full blown job. We waved goodbye as I walked toward the door.

"Do you need a ride, Brina?"

I turned around. "Nope. It's a beautiful night to walk home."

I unlocked the door from the inside and locked it again with my key from the outside. The night was still and quiet. I only walked down the street for a minute when I heard someone whistle from behind me. My sister sat on top of her new car she dubbed a "wicked pissa." The little red bug was handed down to me, even though I preferred to walk rather than take the car places. I hadn't seen my sister since she left for the university a few months ago. A giant smile adorned both our faces. I ran back toward her and wrapped her up in a hug.

"How did you know I was here?"

Estella motioned for me to get into the passenger seat. "I got home early. Mom and dad told me you were still working for kooky Reba."

I smiled. "Yeah, I like working with her."

Estella put on her signal light to make her way back into traffic. Her little car leaned as she banged a uey toward the highway. "I'm cruising for time. Can you tell?"

I laughed, thoroughly enjoying this new relationship I had with my sister. "You missed me that much?"

My sister grinned. "How have you been?"

Shrugging, I replied, "I'm living."

"Do you…you know…miss him?"

I had a hole in my heart where he had taken the piece with him. Of course, I missed him. He was what I thought of first thing in the morning and right before bed. I stalked him on the internet, the television, and the paper tabloids. I regretted letting him go as I did, but I didn't regret the reason why I let him go. That didn't mean I didn't want him back. Confucius couldn't be any more confusing than me. Dylan had a movie that would set him up for the rest of his life. It would have been selfish of me to let him give that up for a whimsical relationship.

"I miss him."

Estella nodded and turned down another street. She

put her signal up to get on the highway. I scrutinized my surroundings, wondering where she was taking me.

"Uh, you do know that home was back there somewhere."

My beautiful older sister shrugged and smiled. "I have somewhere I want to take you."

I couldn't fathom where we were going, but I got comfortable and enjoyed the ride. The night was clear and warm enough to have the window down. The lights of the city got closer as we neared the downtown city district. On this side of town, the world was unlike our small town. Estella took an exit and drove us toward the international airport. Now, where the heck were we going? I turned to look at my sister, who gave nothing away.

Her phone rang.

"Hi, baby. Yeah, I'm home for the weekend. You coming too, right?"

I could hear my sister and Stefan talk about their plans to meet over the long weekend. A large university in the Midwest offered Stefan a contract to play football. My sister went to the local university only a few hours away from us, but preferred to live on campus. They may have been states apart, but that didn't stop them from finding time for one another. Estella had gone months without seeing Stefan, but she handled it like a pro. Sometimes I wished I would have done the same thing with Dylan. I was sure he would never talk to me again. I broke his heart. It turned out that I was worse for him than any other woman he had dated before me.

We pulled down another airport exit. "Where are we going, Estella?"

She sighed. "I'm not the only one that thinks you both must be miserable right now."

"What?"

"Don't hate me, but I went through hell to find June's number."

My heart flipped. "You did what?"

Estella took another turn toward the private airport beside the larger one.

"I called June because you were miserable, and I needed to know if he was too."

I didn't like that my sister had gone behind my back, but I couldn't say that I wasn't as curious as her. "What did June say?"

My sister took another turn. This lane led us down a private road, and at the end of the way was a gated entry and a security booth.

"June told me Dylan has buried himself in his work for the past six months. He refused to talk to anyone about the break-up."

I held my breath as we approached the guard. "Hi. We're Estella and Brina Palace. I believe you received a call to give us access by Juniel Taylor-Lemore's secretary?"

The guard studied his paperwork and nodded. He opened the gate to let us through. "Please stay down the lined road only."

Estella smiled and drove through the open gate. "Anyway, he's done filming for a bit and was getting back home to the hub today. June said Dylan was set to arrive at this airport from his private jet in about another ten minutes."

My weak heart wailed, so I clutched a hand to my chest to stop it from ripping through my clothes. What was I going to do here? What did I think? That Dylan Marcus would forgive me and take me back?

"This is a mistake, Estella. I said some nasty things to him. He doesn't want to see me."

"I get that you did this for his benefit, but you can't just go by what that bitch Vanessa said. Try talking to him. Don't give up on him just like that."

Just as Estella parked her car, a white plane approached the airport from the west. We neared the small lit-up building where pilots and clients rested in-between flights. Estella cooed. I wanted to throw up.

My sister came around and held my hand. "Do it, Brina. Tell him the truth. The one thing I've always admired about you is your unwavering faith and honesty. Show him who Brina Palace truly is."

Sucking in a deep breath, I watched the plane land and slowly reached the front of the building. A couple of people walked out of the building and toward the plane. There was a large chain-link fence that blocked half of the building. One half was on the side the vehicles traversed, while the other side was near the planes. The door to the aircraft opened, and some of Dylan's entourage came off first. I put a hand to my throat. Could I do this? Could I go up to him and beg for forgiveness?

Then he was there.

Marcus stood at the top of the staircase with an arm stretched over his head. He seemed so different, yet so familiar to me. I knew they had cut his hair for the role

Dylan played, but seeing him so tired and gruff wasn't something I was used to seeing. He cared about how he looked. Even on his days off, when Marcus didn't want to shave, he would let his beard grow out. However, he always managed to keep it tamed. Right now, Dylan was a wild mess who had come back from the Amazon, and he still managed to look sexier to me. I didn't even hear Estella call out to me. I ran toward the doors. As I opened the door on my end, Marcus walked through the door on his side. I stopped, out of breath, and stared at the man I had fallen in love with over text.

Dylan nodded at something one of the women said and looked up. His eyes caught mine, and he stopped. The person behind him slammed into him, and the woman beside him stared at each one of us. I saw his eyebrows come together. He was getting angry. I needed to get this off my chest before I lost my nerve.

"I'm sorry."

The woman beside him gasped. The man behind him glanced around Dylan Taylor's shoulder to see what was going on. Dylan didn't say anything. He stood there like a beautiful carved-out sculpture.

The man leaned in. I heard him whisper, "Do you need us to call security?"

I wanted to die of mortification. The truth needed to come out before security escorted me out. "I lied to you. I told you I fell for the characters you played, and that wasn't true. I fell in love with you. So much so that I needed to break up with you so that you could continue to spread your wings and challenge yourself to more."

Dylan blinked but otherwise didn't show me he was paying my speech any attention.

I didn't care and continued. "I knew you were going to give up that role for me, and I couldn't allow you to do that. I also knew that if we waited for one another while you finished the role, then you wouldn't give it your best. We'd both be miserable waiting to hear from one another that we'd both lose focus—you with your roles and me with school."

I wiped at the tears that fell from my eyes. "I'm sorry I lied. I lied to you and lied to myself. When Vanessa told me about this role, I knew that I couldn't let you let it slip through your fingers. I loved you way too much to let that happen. I'm sorry."

He stayed quiet for a long time. So long, that I sighed and went to turn around. I had lost him completely.

"You broke my heart," he called out.

I heard those four words, and more tears fell from my eyes. "I know. I don't deserve you."

"I missed you so much."

My eyes sought his, and I felt a slight hint of hope. "I missed you too. More than you know."

He took a couple of steps toward me. "What would make you think that this was the only way to go our separate ways?"

I wiped at a lone tear with the back of my hand. "I'm an idiot. I figured I was selfish. You belonged to me, but I had to share you with the rest of the world."

Dylan laughed. "Gosh, you're so foolish, Brina Palace."

I nodded.

"But that's what I love about you."

Words caught in my throat. Before I could say something, Dylan had finished walking the rest of the way and captured my lips with his own. I relished the feel of him on my lips. Wrapping my arms around him, I pulled him closer to me. Dylan had both his hands on my face. He kissed me like a parched man in search of water. The people around us clapped. There was a time when I thought the fairytale ending had nothing to do with me. But that's because I never imagined I'd have a fairytale ending like this one. The one that belonged to me and me only. My ending was with the man of my dreams.

With the man on the other end of the line.

Dylan Marcus Taylor

THE CAMERAS FLASHED around me, and this time I smiled like I genuinely meant it because I did. I didn't have to fake it in front of the cameras anymore. Over a year ago, I would have walked on the red carpet and faked a smile for the cameras and fans that had come out to watch my movies. Today, I walked the same red carpet but couldn't contain the joy on my face. My latest film, War of Hearts, had received high critic reviews and ratings before it had even aired in the states. I was ecstatic that this film was what I needed in my life. I stood on the red carpet for the movie's premiere in Los Angeles with my beautiful girlfriend beside me.

Brina smiled up at me, and I fell in love with her all over again. She was radiant in the long, pale pink, Cinderella-type gown she wore and the black and pink chucks she hid underneath. When my heart beat a staccato, and my fingers itched to touch her, I realized I *could* fall more in love with her at any moment. Brina had graduated high school and planned to go to business school to open up her own online business. Bree wanted others to find love just like we did. Her interest in application development gave her the idea of creating a software program that would use messenger to communicate with someone entirely at random. The plan would be able to allow the client options to seek love, friendship, or both.

I pressed my woman closer to me. With a hand on her chin, I lifted her face to mine. Leaning in, I pressed my lips to hers.

I whispered against her lips, "I love you, Brina Palace."

She smiled against my lips as flashes of light momentarily blinded us.

I had accidentally met the woman of my dreams, and I couldn't have been happier. This moment was how my life should be. We walked farther down the carpet and posed for more pictures. My co-star, Vanessa, stood in front of us. She smiled and winked. I had hated Vanessa for digging into my life as she did, but I was also grateful to her for her interference. If she hadn't talked to Bree, then we wouldn't have broken up, and I would have missed on the role of a lifetime.

Brina waved to a few reporters and smiled. She was becoming a pro at the schmoozing game. I laughed, and she sought out my face with those full, green almond-shaped eyes.

"You have my heart, Brina Palace. Marry me."

She smiled and kissed me. "Now, what did I tell you about being a bully?"

I laughed and wrapped my arms around the small woman who drove me crazy in love. She didn't answer me with words, but the adoration on her face gave me my answer. The cameras flashed around us, documenting my blissful happiness. This was the movie of my life. This scene was the role I was always meant to play.

Right here.

Right now.

With Bree.

Acknowledgments

This being the very first book I'd written ever, the acknowledgments section would've been pretty bland. When I first wrote The Other End of the Line, I wanted to read a book about something similar and couldn't find one at the time. I said to myself, "Why not write it?" So, I did, after loads of procrastinating. It took me years to finish this book, and when I finally released it to the world, I realized I was not as good at English as I thought. My story was riddled with mistakes. It looked like one big 'ol mess, but people still read it and enjoyed it. I recall one lousy rating on Goodreads, which made me go back one more time to the story and work on remedying the issue. I am re-publishing this book four years after publishing it but with the help this time.

I give all the love to my favorite, most talented book cover artist. Andrea is amazing. She does all my covers for every book I've had published. Thank you for once again bringing my story to life with your creativity.

Thank you, ladies, at MK, for enjoying the story, even past the mess. To my fantastic editor, Martha, and her team at MK Editing whose diligence made things happen. Without her exceptional skills, I would not have been able to fix the plethora of mistakes with which this book had.

I'd also like to send a shout out to Moms Who Write, a Facebook group that has helped me with moral support and fantastic advice throughout my journeys.

Lastly, my family and God get my last acknowledgments. I wouldn't have been able to do it without them. My husband for pushing me to write it, and my beautiful daughter for loving the story so much. She's read it three times, and each time falls more and more in love with the characters. She always tells me, "Mom, thanks for writing that limo scene *wink*."

More Books by Lyna Lopez

Project Hercules
Trilogy

The Rayne Project

The Black Widow

The Seaa Finale

L y n a   L o p e z

has an obsession with reading stories that separate her from the real world and writing about fantastical places and things. She loves watching Asian dramas and anime whenever she can. For a while, she taught children with emotional, behavioral disabilities, and in-between grading assignments and curbing behavior, she earned her Bachelors in English Literature with Grand Canyon University and her Masters in Creative Writing with Southern New Hampshire University, as well as writing articles for The Odyssey Online. Now, Lyna spends as much time as she can writing books that can transport her readers to whole new worlds. She lives on a mini-farm in Florida with her four crazy kids, rascal-of-a-husband, five wacky dogs, three prissy cats, and all the chickens and ducks—cows coming soon.

@lynalopezsauthor

www.lynalopez.com

www.ingramcontent.com/pod-product-compliance
Lightning Source LLC
Chambersburg PA
CBHW011148190726
48288CB00010B/3229